ERICA MOU (Apulia, 1990) studied Literature, Publishing and Journalism at the University of Bari. She is an Italian singer-songwriter who has won numerous international awards. *Thirsty Sea*, winner of the Readers Award of the Lungano Literary Festival 2020, is her debut novel. Erica wrote this book in the kitchen of her rented accommodation in London.

CLARISSA BOTSFORD grew up in the UK and holds degrees in Modern Languages and Comparative Education. She moved to Rome as an English lector and ended up staying. A taste for literary translation developed later in life, having worked in the fields of journalism, publishing, non-fiction translation, inter-cultural education and training. Clarissa has translated numerous authors from Italian, including Elvira Dones, Viola Ardone, Alessandro Baricco, Concita De Gregorio, Sacha Naspini and Lia Levi. She is also a musician and a humanist celebrant.

Erica Mou

Thirsty Sea

TRANSLATED FROM THE ITALIAN
BY CLARISSA BOTSFORD

HÉ/OÏSE

PRESS

First published in English in Great Britain in 2022 by
Héloïse Press Ltd
4 Pretoria Road
Canterbury CT1 1QL

www.heloisepress.com

First published under the original Italian language title *Nel mare c'è la sete*
© 2020 Fandango Libri s.r.l.

This translation © Clarissa Botsford 2022

Cover design by Laura Kloos
Copy-edited by Lucy Rand
Text design and typesetting by Tetragon, London
Printed and bound in Great Britain by CPI Group (UK) Ltd, Croydon, CRO 4YY

This work has been translated with support from the Centre for Books and Reading of the Italian Ministry of Culture

"SUMMERTIME"
Words and Music by Du Bose Heyward, George Gershwin, Ira Gershwin and Dorothy Heyward © 1935 Ira Gershwin Music (GMR), all rights on behalf of Ira Gershwin Music administered by Warner Geo Met Ric Music

ISBN 978-1-7397515-0-0

CENTRO
PER IL LIBRO
E LA LETTURA

To Lusi

You have the green thumb
I water the plants

ALESSANDRO PAPPOLLA

CONTENTS

Beyond Translation

I was thrilled to be asked by Héloïse Press to translate their first women-in-translation project, *Thirsty Sea*. Erica Mou is an Italian indie singer-songwriter and she uses the same kind of musical and lexical creativity in her writing as she does in her other work. There is melody, harmony and a constant attention to the impact, significance and intentionality of language.

Maria, the narrative voice – ironic, deeply human, with all her flaws, linguistic tics and curiosities, and her talent for turning life's questions back to front in a form of relentless self-accusation – is the theme tune, which plays throughout the novel with variations and fugues. The ground bass is an ostinato of guilt, on a loop for the twenty-four hours into which the novel is compressed, relentlessly returning to the same inescapable question of culpability. The harmony is provided by the past and the future that weave in and out of Maria's relentless present, and by the repeated, almost obsessive interjections of her thoughts: an imminent decision for the future, an agonising reckoning with the past, which is constantly interrupted, postponed, procrastinated, in what amounts to an interminable and almost irritating avoidance mechanism.

Just as lyrics are an essential component of songs, so are words in this novel modulated, manipulated and moulded to fit the theme tune. They are called upon to reinforce, with their own internal paradoxes and meanings, with their own rhythm and timbre, the novel's message. Challenges for the translator are trip-wired into the text and the musical structure. And this is where my experience of translating *Thirsty Sea* has been unique. Not only was Aina Martí-Balcells, the publisher, intimately involved in the process – alongside Lucy Rand, copy-editor supreme and translator in her own right – but I was also privileged to meet Erica Mou on two separate occasions: once on Zoom and once 'in real life' at my home, where we worked creatively together on how to dodge the booby traps that she had (involuntarily?) set for her translator.

The main translation issue is Maria's (and Erica's) fixation with words that contain other words, compound words and double meanings in words. The way we transformed the text was truly a trans-creation. In many cases, the translation we ended up being happy with bore no relation whatsoever to the original. What was so liberating for me as a translator was the author saying to me as we jiggled words around: 'It's my text. We can do what we like with it.' And we did. It was like juggling plates: it requires great skill, it's mesmerising, and it's scary.

Mou, like her protagonist Maria, lived in London for a period (and wrote much of this novel there). Her command of English is excellent. At the same time, as a non-native speaker – and as a songwriter – she has an original way of approaching individual words, untrammelled by the rules of usage or collocation. Add to this a strong grounding in the Classics and therefore of etymology, a razor-sharp wit, hawk-eye precision, a penchant for irony and a tendency to play word games at all times.

Every chapter has a postscript: a 'title word' and a short poem. The 'title word' is related to the content, message or significance of the section, while the short poem is related to the meaning of one or both parts of the word. In some instances, we changed the word, in others we changed the poem and rewrote it from scratch to match the word, in others again we were inspired to change both, in Mou's words, 'improving on the original'. 'This word has been left behind compared to the others we've already worked on,' she would say. And off we would go, brainstorming and throwing things in the air.

Here are a couple of concrete examples to give a better idea of the process.

The section just before Maria explains why this particular day is such an important anniversary for her is entitled *Arcobaleno*. Luckily for the translator, the English translation, 'rainbow', happens to contain two words: rain and bow. However, less luckily for the translator, in the poem Erica Mou riffs on the meaning *arco* (arch or bow) and *baleno* (*balenare* means to flash but it sounds like *balena*, a whale). The whale conjures up the sea, a constant undercurrent in the book reflected in the title, as well as Pinocchio, who is swallowed by a whale in the Italian childhood staple, and who notoriously lies. The poem also explores the repeated themes of colour, tricks of light and photography (Maria's mother's eyes snapping pictures of her, capturing her guilt in a still that will last forever), and of an impossible treasure that can never be reached. We kept 'Rainbow' as the 'title word' and adapted the poem, introducing a *bow*head whale, a flash and an arch to keep some of the intention of the Italian as well as rain, of course: 'You flash through my mind/ as unwieldy in the ocean/ as a bowhead whale/ You've spat out Pinocchio and stomached his lies/ You flash through my mind/ in every uncatchable hue/ Rainbows never come out in photos, you do/ You flash an arch/ My face embellished by light/ Out of the blue/ in a second of rain/ you go from sea to sky/ But the treasure is hidden on the earth.'

By contrast, between two sections where Maria has some reckonings coming, we changed the 'title word' and kept the text of the poem. The original Italian title is *falsariga* (pattern), which contains the words *falsa* (false) and *riga* (literally 'line', though *mettere in riga* means setting something or somebody straight). The poem is just one line – 'There's no such thing as a horizon' – and we decided to replace the 'title word' *falsariga* with the compound word 'deadline' in order to maintain the idea of a line (horizon) that doesn't exist because it is hidden within a word that means 'time limit'. At the same time, however, we were adding an extra nuance: the menace of the word 'dead' (no spoilers, but Maria's imminent decision implies both a time limit and a death of sorts, while her sister's death definitely clouds every decision she makes).

Finally, there were times when we changed both the 'title word' and the poem, and we ended up paring the English down to the essential… to a far greater extent, in fact, than Mou had in the Italian. *Toccasana* is a remedy, and the word contains *tocca* (touch) and *sana* (meaning both healthy and sane). A literal translation of the original poem would be, 'They are so small you really need to want to read them/the contraindications.' Our final version was: 'Painkiller: side effects are printed too small.' The darker meanings behind *pain* and *killer* speak for themselves, yet the original meaning of 'cure' is retained.

The only problem was that we kept on finding new possibilities, and in the nights that followed our creative day together, I'd wake up with a start – a new compound word with infinite possibilities had just flashed through my mind and I'd have to write it down before it vanished.

This experience of trans-creating has spoiled me for the future, I'm sure of it, but I am grateful for the opportunity this novel has given me to stretch my translating practice to the limits, and I sincerely hope Erica Mou will come up with more surprises in the future.

CLARISSA BOTSFORD

PART ONE

Dinner

Wellspring

Dashing for shelter
in a surprise shower

There's an exact spot on my way home where I open my bag and get my keys out.

Like swimmers when they come to the end of their last lap, stretch an arm out, grab the edge, lift their goggles, turn and look at their time on the scoreboard.

I think about swimmers every day, here, in this same spot, as I rummage in my bag. Hesitating when I should be hurrying, I drag my feet so I can hear my sluggish steps and scream out to the world with the shuffling of my boots that I've arrived, but that I don't want to have arrived.

I stop in front of the door and wish I smoked.

I clasp the keys in my hand and observe them as they rub together noisily. If there were only one of them, I wouldn't hear a thing.

Nicola is up there waiting for me. We always say, I'm upstairs, come up, though we actually live on the ground floor because I don't want to be over anybody's head and I made that clear as soon as we decided to live together.

That you can stack plates but not lives.

Not to mention threehundredandsixtyfive empty exchanges about how time flies faster every year, which floor are you going to, OK, so I'd better get in first.

Maria and Nicola, these are our names, like our grandparents before us and our grandparents' grandparents before us, for ever and ever amen, in the name of the non-evolution of the species.

When I stop torturing the keys, I reach under my scarf and play with a pendant I've worn around my neck for almost thirty years, which my archetype Maria gave me. It's a gold knot, a kind of twenty-four-carat pretzel. Yellow gold. Very yellow. Because family jewels are yellower than others, and heavier, too. In my view. And they don't make a noise. I stand there listening, but there's no sound.

Maybe it's the weight of this necklace that is slowing me down, a few feet from my house, our house.

An ugly building thrown together in haste.

I feel cold. In springtime, in the evenings, though I don't want to believe it, it's cold.

My hands are killing me and the time has come to go in.

Out of the front door comes a woman I don't know, but maybe I should know, with a dog. When we moved here, I thought I would bake enough cakes to feed the whole building and end world hunger, that I would take care of our neighbours' cats and dogs and parrots and goldfish and leave reports on their answering machines when they were away, that I would go around knocking on doors when I ran out of salt.

Instead, I've stuffed every summons to a residents' meeting into the letter box next to mine, labelled Eleonora Marelli. Could she be the woman with the dog?

And whenever I've run out of salt, I've simply gone to the supermarket. Who runs out of salt, anyway? If I counted the number of packets of salt I've bought in my life, I'd maybe get to three. How can you not realise the salt is running out, given the exceptional nature of the event?

Meanwhile, they're holding the door open for me, the woman and the dog, which means I no longer have an excuse, I have to go in.

Great, no need for key number one.

I look at the letter box. At a glance it looks empty, thank goodness.

I walk down the hall and I hear laughter or, more precisely, I hear Nicola laughing from behind the door of our apartment.

Of his laughs, this actually sounds like the real one. He has two: one that comes out in bursts and makes his shoulders shudder, and a long, high laugh with a kind of hole in the middle, interrupted every now and again by a silent sucking in, like an air pocket.

There it is, I hear it, the hole in his laughter.

I love that suspension.

The evening we met, Nicola and I, we were in a bar, what a cliché.

He was gesticulating too much. He was talking too much. He was drinking too little. And I decided to talk to him to interrupt the series of excesses.

'You're making me want to throw up.'

'Sorry? What was that?'

'You move too much. You're like a film with special effects.'

'Don't look at me, then.'

'OK.'

'… Sorry, do films with special effects make you want to throw up?'

'Yeah.'

'Would you like a drink?'

'Yeah.'

'You jumped at that pretty quick.'

'Very.'

'Try this grappa, it's good.'

'Mmm.'

'So do you always accept drinks from strangers without saying a word?'

'What am I supposed to say?'

'Well, didn't you learn the magic word? G-R-A-…'

'… P-P-A.'

And that was when I heard it the first time, that air pocket in the middle of his laugh, like the moment you go over the edge on a roller coaster, when your whole chest is compressed and for a second it feels impossible that it could contain your heart and your lungs and all the things that matter.

I stand a little longer outside the door and I hear another, different, laugh.

Nicola is laughing with someone.

There are people laughing in my house. OK. No, not OK at all.

I'd like to open the door and find someone new, swim up to them, hold out my hand for the first time and say nice to meet you, before gripping onto the edge of their life, like swimmers on their final lap.

Instead, I already know. I already know everything.

I decide to ring the doorbell, good riddance to key number two.

They stop laughing, two sets of steps, restrained but noisy, come my way.

She opens the door.

'Hello, darling!'

'Hi, Mà.'

'You look tired.'

'Which is a kind way of saying I look like shit.'

'No, apricot, you just look tired. Beautiful and tired.'

She kisses me. She hugs me. I hug her. My mother can't cook a thing, and yet her neck always smells like fresh bread straight out of the oven, like warm biscuits.

Biscuits. I love that word.

The table is laid for three. For fuck's sake.

Now she'll say she just happened to be in the neighbourhood, that Nicola and I work too hard, that my father's busy, that it's an impromptu dinner.

And we'll all pretend that everything's fine. Except Nicola won't be pretending because he really doesn't get it, because, every year without fail, he forgets what fucking day it is today.

Goalkeeper

Anything you let in, gets to you

Today it's twenty-five years since I killed my sister.

Nobody has ever said it out loud, but I can hear other people's thoughts loud and clear. And the unmanageable ones have a special sound: they make a slow constant rumble like waves crashing against docks, like high heels as you carry on walking, resisting and smiling.

My mother says that it wasn't my fault.

My mother wears them often, high heels, that is.

That we shouldn't use paper towels as napkins. Is what she's saying in the meantime, before I've shrugged my jacket off.

Nicola nods, adding yet another ladle of broth to the pan.

That risotto should be eaten on flat plates, not in bowls, she always says. That once she and my father ate a risotto with strawberries and he thought it was disgusting, she says.

They laugh, together. About the fact that fruit should be treated as fruit.

I go to the toilet and sit there for a long time, even after I'm done.

I think about the seasons, the tides, the precession of the equinoxes, the full moon, hibernation, flowers.

And then there's us, our life marked by a succession of meals. Nothing else.

I look at the toilet paper.

I know Nicola is angry with me because I came in without saying hello to him, which means without kissing him, which means he's one of those people who cares about form. But the form of what?

And this evening I have a revelation that maybe caring about form means caring about the stencil, the biscuit cutter, the ready-shaped template of how things should be. Meaning, his attention to form is not just a matter of aesthetics. It's a trail to follow.

It looks like there are still quite a few ladles of broth on the way so I make my way to the living room-studio-bunker, which is my favourite room in the house.

Tomorrow I have two clients before going to my doctor's appointment, and I'm unprepared across the board. What board, I ask myself?

I turn the computer on and think that nights have a way of being very long. In the meantime, I hear my mother and Nicola confabulate in the kitchen, talking about me as if I can't hear them. Though they know perfectly well that I know that they know that I can hear them. They're saying I don't eat enough, that coffee is not food, that my new haircut suits me, even though I'm still shedding clumps of it, that I earn too little and work too much, that I'm always thinking about others but never about myself, that I should have finished university, and on they go, a repeat performance.

Tonight, too, they've run out of tickets.

And we've run out of options, I think, and feel like laughing. My laugh has no suspension.

'It's ready!' they shout.

'Isn't Pà coming?' I provoke.

'Unfortunately he couldn't, darling.'

No reaction. I'm being a bitch but they never realise.

The steaming plates look wonderful.

Lucky them. If I smoked like they do, I'd be able to fill up dead moments, rather than inflicting physical pain on them.

The risotto looks wonderful because Nicola really cares about form, as we've said. And it's delicious, too, as my mother won't fail to point out, between ten and twenty times a minute.

What a treasure your boyfriend is, she reminds me. Bare skin is not enough, we should embellish it at any cost, I think, as I start playing with my twenty-four-carat pendant-pretzel again.

I don't have any tattoos, since life takes care of that on its own, what with coming off your bike, an old smallpox vaccination which shows your age, chicken pox blisters you couldn't resist scratching, sharp corners on bits of furniture, a frying pan that was minding its own business but was still scorching hot.

Not to mention your belly button, the only visible scar produced by a separation.

While the other losses sit there in silence, in front of a steaming hot dish like a smoking gun.

Breakwater

Thirsty sea
never rely on how much there is

Nicola is self-made. He paid his own way through university, and then he took out a loan and got himself a pilot's licence.

Nicola is the kind of person who doesn't kill spiders but catches them in jars and frees them out of the window.

He's taller than average, more handsome than average, and even though I've never seen him do it, I'm sure he helps old ladies cross the street. That he gets up for them on the bus I have actually witnessed.

Nicola irons cotton handkerchiefs, sews buttons on before they drop off, lifts the toilet seat and then puts it back down again, smiles when he looks at you.

My mother sings the praises of this brilliant man all the time, repeats that he's perfect, we're perfect together.

We won each other, as if at an auction.

Liquidate

I don't think we are like good wine
that correctly inclined
we will age well over time
I think, rather, we are like
alcohol and coffee cream
in a badly mixed liquor
Little by little your flavour will separate from mine

'Anna, shall I pour you some more wine?'

'You're always so attentive, Nicola.'

It's no use. My mother just can't bring herself to say Yes or No.

'Are you planning on doing anything for Easter?' says Nicola, who force-feeds silence with words.

'Some friends of ours are going to Marseilles, you know? Maybe Peppe and I will go with them, since we've never been. It's perfect, you know. They're going by car and there are two free places, so I can avoid flying this time, too.'

'How many times do I have to tell you, Anna, flying is much safer than driving.'

'Never enough times, dear Nicola! If I can avoid planes, I happily will. Anyway, Marseilles is lovely, they say, and these friends are experts because—'

'Who are they?' I interrupt, my mouth full.

'Roberta and Franco.'

'Ah, and they are…?'

'Friends from buraco club, mine and Papà's. Alessia's parents. You remember Alessia, right? She was at middle school with you, in another class. You went on a school trip together once. You're the same age, you see?'

'No, I don't.' I swallow. 'So, are you going on holiday with them or not?'

'Papà doesn't mind the idea.'

It's pointless. She just can't do it.

Maybe she has a problem with monosyllables.

My father is like a stone, my mother washes around him.

Her name could only have been Anna, which is the same both ways round.

I think Marseilles is perfect for her: soap and rats.

My mother doesn't expose herself.

She doesn't yell and she doesn't whisper, she talks.

She doesn't despair and she doesn't leap for joy, she weaves through the middle.

She has never told Nicola to use the familiar *tu* with her, but she insists he calls her Anna because if he called her *Signora* it would make her feel old, and because he's family.

She never goes out on a limb, my mother. She simply is.

I don't know whether we are born blank and little by little we colour ourselves in, or whether we come into this world painted in brilliant hues and then we become different shades of grey, but I do know for sure that my mother is pearl, pewter, slate and lead.

One evening many years ago, I was doing my homework on the kitchen table.

I was in my first year of primary school, and I'd taken over the room with pens, pencils, felt tips, glue, highlighters, scissors, exercise books, doing my best as usual to occupy all the available space. I'd worn my hairband so often it was loose, and it kept slipping down over my eyes. So I held my blue pen in one hand, and my hairband in the other.

That's the first photo I remember my mother taking of me, with her eyes.

This is what she does. Every now and again, she looks at things so intensely that she holds them in her head, immobilises them in her thoughts. I've known about this private album of hers for years.

We've never had very many real photos. Hanging on the walls of my parents' house there are mostly film posters and framed cross-stitch samplers.

When my mother takes a picture with her eyes, her face turns greyer, more slate and lead than usual.

Hers is a face that laughs and cries at the same time, that has no direction, like her name.

And so I think that maybe we are born blank. And we forge our path with dashes of bright colour.

But every now and again, an experience is thrown at us that darkens the colours, deepens the layers of grey. Then, when we're ready, we try and lighten them again.

I think my mother must have layered so many dark shades of grey that she was unable to find a bucket of whitewash big enough to repaint herself. She ended up pearl, pewter, slate and lead.

And when, with her flashing eyes, she takes a picture of the world, I can see it.

I can see heaviness stifling joy.

I can see light buoying sadness.

'Well, I think it'll do you good to go,' I say to her.

She scrunches up her nose, narrowing her eyes slightly. Which means she's happy I've said it but sad that we won't be having Easter together.

'So, darling, have you remembered who Alessia is?'

'No, Mà. I haven't.'

Bubblebath

Men and women live together
bubble bath for two
Men and women marry
a child for two
But they go around the world
smelling different

Everyone's plates are empty now. The glasses aren't, though.

We'll have to wait.

'Anna, unfortunately we don't have much else in the house. If I'd known you were coming, I'd have made dessert. I have this new recipe with almonds that's the best. A colleague shared it with me. There's hardly any sugar in it and...'

Blablablablablablablablablablabla.

When people start talking about recipes, I put my ears on flight mode. Boring.

There's always a moment during dinner when someone around the table starts reciting a recipe.

The redundancy of talking about food while you're eating is something I'll never understand.

Every time, I imagine these ladies, these Nicolas, these aunts and uncles, these grandmothers in aprons, standing up in the middle of the meal, climbing onto a chair and reciting, like kids with a Christmas poem.

Except those kids are prompted by others and, thank God, sometimes they are too embarrassed to go through with it and run to their bedrooms. A nice way of refusing to be performing monkeys and telling adults to piss off.

Grown-up recipe reciters, however, do it on their own. Grown-up recipe reciters are never embarrassed.

Pancake

Force of habit
is the greatest weakness

To tell the truth, though, this compound word game in my head is the imaginary chair I stand on, from which I recite my thoughts when I need to disengage (what a good word) from my existence. I really love words that contain other words, when they are simultaneously the same but new.

At primary school, my teacher told us that the Dolomite Alps used to be a seabed. And I don't think I ever recovered from that knowledge.

The sea turning into a mountain.

And if the sea can turn into a mountain, what's the point of starting a sentence with the words: 'I'm someone who…'? There's never anyone who surprises you with a nice, 'I'm this and that and an infinite range of other possibilities.'

I really don't know what I am. You try describing your-selves with only three adjectives, if you dare, dear HR people with your ready-made job interviews.

Rain and bows are two different things, but together they form something new, like man and drill, or dog and fish.

But this chair is mine and mine only, in my own head, and I try not to bore anyone else when I climb up on it.

'… bake it for twenty minutes at 180 degrees and ta-da.'

'Yum, that sounds delicious. Next time, maybe. Today I brought dessert, though… something Maria goes mad over. Wait, I hid it in the hall cupboard!'

There you go, my mother is unbeatable in this area.

She never forgets. Ever.

There it is on the horizon, in her hands, perfect in its shimmering wrapper, like a butterfly, a bit of blue, a patch of fuchsia, a touch of every colour: Her Majesty the Easter Egg.

Dark chocolate 75%. Contains a luxury surprise.

'Thanks, Mà.'

'You're welcome, apricot.'

Snap.

She takes one of her pictures with her eyes, my mother does, while the egg changes hands from hers to mine.

And I hear the snap. So loud that my instinct is to make a face, to ruin the image for her.

'I thought I'd bring it to you today, you know… so that if Papà and I do go to France in the end… Well, I don't know if you want to open it now or if you'd prefer to wait until Sunday.'

'I'll wait until Sunday.'

'OK.'

Nicola is uninterested, and starts clearing the table because, when it comes to chocolate, he and I are different.

From a certain age onwards, sugar in coffee and milk chocolate should be outlawed. He disputes this, saying that I don't appreciate life's pleasures, and I answer that he may be right but if it were me making the laws, he'd know what bitterness was.

I yawn in a slightly exaggerated fashion and my mother, the pewter, slate and lead wave, says, as she gulps down the last of her wine, 'Well, it's getting late. So, dears, if Peppe and I go away, we'll catch you next week, OK? Maybe Tuesday.'

'Oh, OK then. Happy Easter.'

'Happy Easter, Anna, goodnight,' says Nicola, holding her scarf.

'Mà...?'

'What, apricot?'

'... say hi to Pà, OK?'

'OK.'

Snap. Again.

And she turns on her heels and closes the door.

It's over. Once again.

We wash up to Sybille Baier singing 'Tonight'. This song wrecks me and Nicola knows it, that's why he puts it on while we're doing the dishes. That way, I concentrate on the anguish in her voice and, in comparison, washing up is a walk in the park.

Every evening we go through the same hackneyed script: we should really get a dishwasher (I like that word), but no, really, it's fine as things are, though it is pretty boring, OK then, let's buy one, right, I'll look online, OK, you look, but maybe it's a waste of money, though time is worth far more than a thousand euros and a two-year guarantee, don't you think? Yes, so let's look. And of course, we never do.

'Don't you think you're too old to get an Easter egg?'

Dear Nicola, do I really have to start explaining to you about the Dolomites and the sea, about possible lives inside one life, about words that contain other words, about all the things in the world that unexpectedly contain something else, about Russian dolls, closed curtains, oysters, about how I always feel, today more than ever?

But I prefer not to get up onto that chair in front of you.

I take my thoughts back into their room.

And with my feet in my stripy slippers firmly planted on the kitchen rug, and a pair of yellow rubber gloves on my hands, I decide to give you an explanation which is false but much more logical according to your criteria of what is logical.

'Of course I am. But it makes my mother happy.'

Slapdash

Force of habit
is my force of gravity

I've come into the bathroom to brush my teeth, which is one of the things I like the most in the universe.

Fresh, immaculate, immune.

Almost ten years ago, I went to London for a holiday, with the intention of never coming back. The intention of never coming back, though, I'd kept to myself, or maybe I'd never actually communicated it to myself because I didn't need to.

Purse, passport, toothbrush. I don't remember putting much else in my suitcase. As if travelling light was an art for which the only things that really count are paying, identifying yourself and brushing your teeth.

Self-sufficiency, legality, dignity.

Clearly, seeing as I had a purse, I could easily have bought myself another toothbrush, but I couldn't risk even for one second feeling that I wasn't fresh, immaculate, immune.

ERICA MOU

Lightness, lightness, lightness, that's what I was looking for.

There was a block of marble in the middle of my chest, between my ribs and my sternum. A block of marble that if you were Michelangelo you could turn into something beautiful, but that in my body was nothing but a block of marble, valuable and useless.

I started with an empty suitcase.

And as I climbed up the steps to the plane, it was so windy I had to cover my face with my hands.

I remember that, when I was a little girl, I used to cry a lot. I threw a tantrum once because I wanted a balloon. One of the few memories I have of myself from when I was that young.

I must have been about five or six.

There were lights strung up and stalls and I was crying and my mother finally gave in and bought it, the star-shaped, polka-dot helium balloon. The man at the stall – I can only remember his hands – tied it around my wrist.

I was proud, for a minute or two.

Then tears welled up in my eyes again, I felt I was suffocating. I opened and shut my hands until I managed to wriggle out of the knot and until, without letting any of the grown-ups see, I was able to let the balloon go.

Up it went, into the sky, growing smaller and smaller as I grew lighter and lighter. I followed it with my gaze, just as I would watch a guest walking down the garden path as I waved goodbye.

We were accomplices, me and my polka-dot star.

But my mother didn't understand and, to make me happy, she bought me another one.

We took it home, I hated it. Every day it shrunk a little.

The first one, instead, by becoming a dot in the sky, had grown huge.

We waited a week before throwing balloon number two away, so shrivelled and sad that at night I was scared to share a room with it. That was the moment I started to want to grow up in a hurry, to have my own purse with my own money, so that I could finally choose not to buy anything for myself.

I don't know whether I ever wanted what I asked for.

I don't think I ever actually asked for anything.

The day I was travelling to the UK, on the steps to the plane there was a lot of wind but, even with an empty suitcase, I was still too heavy for it to move me.

When I got to London, in the kitchen of the hostel I was staying in I met Ruth, a girl with ears full of silver rings, who was heating up something yellow in the microwave. She smiled a lot and I thought that she, too, must really care about dental hygiene.

Maybe Ruth, like me, put money, passport and a tooth-brush into her suitcase first. She told me she travelled a lot and often on her own, all over the world, and she couldn't imagine anything better.

So, maybe her white teeth served to show everybody how happy travelling made her.

Or maybe it was so she would always be ready to be immortalised, because you never know when someone might take a picture of you, either for real or with their eyes, like my mother does.

'Ruth, do you know how to sculpt?'

'What do you mean?'

'I mean, would you be able to sculpt a statue from a piece of stone?'

'No, but I do know how to draw up birth charts. I'll do yours for seven pounds, if you like.'

'Thanks, but no thanks. But would you like a coffee from the machine?'

'OK.'

We blew on our plastic cups, it was hot. Cheers.

'Ruth, what do you think pain teaches you?'

'That suffering sucks.'

We smiled with yellow teeth, but only from the coffee.

I come out of the bathroom wearing my pyjamas.

Nicola is under the duvet, setting a string of alarms three minutes apart on his phone. I slip under the covers and he puts one arm around my neck and strokes my belly with the other.

I move away.

'What's wrong, Mary Mine?'

'Sorry, it hurts.'

'Period?'

'Yep.'

'Oh no… already?'

It's not true, I don't have my period. I said it so he would leave me alone.

Every evening when I go to bed I feel anxious because I know he'll want to make love.

'Did you feed Antongiulio?' I ask.

'No, it was your turn today.'

'Really? Well, never mind. We'll make it up to him tomorrow.'

'But he'll die of hunger!'

We laugh, kind of.

Antongiulio is our imaginary dog.

A real one, with four busy legs and fur and musty breath and a tail, in our apartment, would be too much. And I don't like small dogs, it feels like cheating. Anyway, everything is easier with an imaginary dog as you always have the option of cumulating meals when you forget. Like those stupid Tamagotchi things, programmed not to actually die in order to avert teenage depression or suicide. All I had to do when my little monster was dying was pull a white tab and reset it so it could be reborn and start life over again.

'Goodnight, Mary Mine.'

Ritual kiss like a rubber stamp.

Hey block of marble, there you are.

I know you haven't gone anywhere, but at night in bed I feel you more keenly, like the ringing in your ears after the disco that you don't realise is there until you lie down in silence.

At night, my perception of it is clearer, this block of marble, this priceless, icy anchor that weighs me down.

And it's obvious that the wind, that day on the plane steps, would never have been able to lift me.

Lopsided

With irregular angles
a kite can't take off

My father has left a press release on the globe.

Maria is on her own. We need someone to look after her.
  Friends, relatives, acquaintances, hurry along now.
  Auditions to be held at Grotta beach at 3 this afternoon.

I start walking to get there on time, before the candidates.

It's a spring day, one of those days that bewitch you with the sun and catch you out with the wind.

I'm wearing a denim jacket and a school bag I had in middle school, covered in faded scribbles in gold marker.

I'm early. The beach is still deserted.

I sit on a solitary rock near the water. I drop my bag and take my jacket off, but I still feel hot so I strip off my sweater and tie it around my waist.

I'm in a one-piece swimming costume split in two by the waistband of my trousers.

I think I could dive in, but I know that on days like these, it's best not to trust the sea. I know that the sea does it on purpose, it looks at you all calm and shimmery and you fall for it and take a sock off. But your big toe, an infallible thermometer, decides that no, it's not time yet, and slips back into your shoe.

It's a waste of time, untying your laces, drying your foot, lacing them up again, when you know right from the start that you really can't trust the sea on a day like this.

No, this time I'm not falling for it, I'm going to stay sitting here half-mermaid half-woman, in silence.

Because I know that even for little mermaid Ariel, gaining legs that allowed her to go around the world on her own cost her her voice.

Minutes go by and nobody turns up.

I put my hand in my pocket and pull out my phone.

It's 3.10 and there's no sign of any of these friends, relatives or acquaintances.

And so, I think, I must have come to the wrong beach. In some other part of the town, on another beach, my future is being played out.

Different versions of my life are being skimmed, like flat stones, into the sea.

The rippling circles get wider and wider and they are more and more mistaken, they must be stopped.

I must leave, find the exact spot, I must stop them. But as I'm getting dressed again, I look up at the horizon and see the most beautiful thing I've ever seen. It's a whole rainbow, one hundred and eighty degrees of bright colours.

When did it rain?

Can there be a rainbow without rain?

I pick up my phone again, I must take a picture of this masterpiece. Everyone must see it. All those summoned to the other beach must see what I've seen here, what they missed.

I take the first, the second, the twentieth picture.

Snap.

It's so beautiful.

But then I suddenly hear a noise, like the sound of a coin spinning fast on a table, of a rotating door, a top.

It's the rainbow that's starting to detach itself from the sky and teeter, like the spinning coin as it loses speed. It's falling, a half hula hoop projecting its shadow on the sea, then on the beach, then on me.

The colours drain out.

It will fall. Because coins and tops, once they stop spinning, always fall.

It will crush everything.

The sea, the beach, the phone, me, the bag, the world.

I wake up with a start.

My computer is still on my lap. I press a key to reactivate the screen, so I have a little light. Just enough to dismiss the end of the world on a deserted beach.

I can just make out Nicola sleeping face down next to me, his arms above his head.

I could pick up a piece of chalk, draw around his outline and secure the crime scene.

The world is still there.

Rainbow

You flash through my mind
as unwieldy in the ocean
as a bowhead whale

You've spat out Pinocchio and stomached his lies

You flash through my mind
in every uncatchable hue
Rainbows never come out in photos, you do

You flash an arch
My face embellished by light

Out of the blue
in a second of rain
you go from sea to sky
But the treasure is hidden on the earth

Summer died twenty-five years ago.

Summer was her name, my sister, that is.

Like my parents' favourite song.

The clearest memory I have of her is the day I killed her, when I saw her peach-pink face turn deep blue, like the sea.

The fact is that my mother's mother and my father's mother, the one that gave me the necklace, were both called Maria. And she, my sister, managed to escape the inherited name. Because she came after me, once the name on my birth certificate had already enabled everyone involved to pay their dues to their reputation, tradition and well-being.

You give us the colour of our eyes, a tongue that can either roll or not, cardiovascular disease, baldness, the shape of our nose, varicose veins.

Why, then? Why do you have to stick our name in too, as if it were part of our DNA?

47

Have a little imagination, parents. Accept a degree of symbolism, have the courage to make a choice.

My parents took responsibility for choosing Summer's name, but not mine.

As different as they are, in the end our names had one thing in common: they both had only one meaning.

Not like Rosalba, Gianbattista or Piergiorgio. What's the point of giving two names to one person? We're not objects – cork-screw, tin-opener, ash-tray – we don't need to be explained.

And anyway, there would never be enough words to colour in and explain a life.

You would need passports in volumes, whole encyclopaedias, and airport controls would go on forever. Best not waste time, best keep things short.

Let's leave objectivity and definitions to inanimate things.

And anyway, what does a name explain?

What destiny does a name bring with it?

None. Absolutely none.

Of the two sisters, in fact, I'm the one who's alive, the one with a biblical name that's been used and reused without ever risking a thing.

Nor do I believe that dying at the age of three is somehow special, summery, long-awaited, holiday-like, or luminous. Or is it?

It's late and I'm tired, so tired that I'm no longer sleepy.

I don't want to fall asleep and be crushed by the sky, again.

The computer is still on my lap. I guess I'll do a bit of work.

Heartthrob

Tick tock
Tick tock
Which wire do you cut
to defuse the bomb?

Summertime, and the livin' is easy…

My mother used to sing and my father used to dance in the sitting room, stepping on her toes.

For the last twenty-five years, though, I don't remember any music in my parents' house, in the house that for many years was mine. Films, yes. Lots of them. My father watched at least one a day, sometimes more, switching the TV off as soon as they'd said the last line.

Before the credits.

He has never given a damn about the names of the actors, the composer of the soundtrack, the editor, the assistant director, or the clips they sometimes show during the credits. Cuts, funny mistakes, or real photos of the people who inspired the film. My father always switched the TV off immediately, just as the final image dissolved into blackness.

My father is interested in substance, what's there and what isn't.

My father doesn't like explanations, he finds them on his own.

When a film comes to an end, he turns to my mother, if she has been watching with him, and says, 'What did you think?'

My mother, at that point, ad-libs a review with a good word for everyone, even abysmal actors and blind directors.

My father never listens, he just nods.

He has never given a damn about other people's opinions, either.

Sandpaper

You can cut yourself
turning pages

Everything hurts after the rainbow crushed me in my dream a few minutes ago. Adding its weight to the block of marble that's always there.

Every year, on this day, I think back to what happened. I try and remember it properly, from start to finish, that day twenty-five years ago, but my memories always come out in tiny multicoloured building bricks.

I've heard it from others, many times: from my mother, from both Marias, my grandmothers, from the psychologist, from the other psychologist, from gossip, from my teachers, from my own voice ricocheting off the mirror. From my father, never.

Reconstructions.

All of them telling me, in a strangled voice, that it wasn't my fault.

My sister, like me, couldn't roll her tongue. Actually, I can't remember that, either.

But it's science, it's a given, it's DNA, and you don't question it.

Watermark

> All you needed to do was pick me up and shine a light
> to see whether I'd ever been there

There's just one sound I remember from that day. One word.

No.

My mother said.

No.

My father said.

In chorus, *forte, fortissimo*.

No. They yelled: No.

Then they said Help and then again, No.

My mother was wailing and clasping and compressing and auscultating and saying, No.

A thousand times.

With my sister tight in her arms she kept saying, No.

She turned her over like a doll, she thumped her on the back, then she hung her upside down by her feet and she kept saying No. Just No.

And that No dissolved everything into layers of grey.

I no longer existed, and then our room no longer existed, and then all the words in the world vanished, except one.

My dead sister was the only thing that seemed to exist.

No.

They came to get her the next day, two men in white gloves.

It all felt very clean.

My father was curled up in a corner, as if he were being

punished. He held his palms up to his face, his hands were rough and so big that it looked as though they were enveloping him. That's how small he'd made himself.

My mother was still repeating that two-letter word, which I've never heard her utter since.

No.

She went on shaking her head, black lines running down her cheeks, her hair stuck to her face. She went on holding Summer's hand, so tight that the white gloves found it hard to break her grip.

My grandmothers were taking care of me, weeping and praying, shuttling me between their respective houses and snacks. The days were full of Marias, I couldn't say how many days there were. Our names and the days were all the same: indivisible.

At that time, I had two homes and two makeshift beds, lots of TV quizzes and fruit juice at all hours. Nobody took me to school, nobody scolded me. Hardly anyone spoke to me and, when they did, they didn't know what to say.

I was waiting for the moment that everything would go back to normal.

My mother didn't speak, she howled and wailed.

My father didn't emit a single sound.

I was waiting for me and everything in the world around me to come back into existence.

We used to call the game *Un, due, tre, stella!*

We'd sneak forward and when the person who was It said 'stella' we'd all freeze, knowing we'd soon be able to run again.

Not long before leaving for London, I found out that the game had nothing to do with stars at all.

One, two, three, *stay there*!

That was the real name of the game and, actually, thinking about it, it made much more sense. It made much more sense and it was much more ugly.

It's often the case, when you're grown up, that the imperatives extinguish the stars.

Bedrock

Spoiler:
Tonight I turn into stone

Thank God for eBay, hallowed be thy name!

I've finally found something that helps me get through the night.

A few days ago, a woman in her fifties came into the shop to buy a present for her boss, who is about to become her ex-boss because he's finally retiring.

These people who refuse to relinquish their posts despite being in a position to do so must be suffering from a chronic dearth of interests.

'What about one of his hobbies?'

'Hobbies? As in pastimes?'

'Exactly.'

'Well, Mr Zaccari doesn't have any, I don't think.'

I knew it.

'Films?'

'Hm... I don't think so. He goes to bed very early.'

'Music?'

'Never heard him listening to any.'

'Sport?'

'He's seventy-four.'

'Right.'

'Anyway, even if he did have any hobbies, I wouldn't like him to think that I consider him old or, worse still, unproductive. His motto is: a day off is a day wasted.'

'Nice.'

'Not really…'

Right, the woman doesn't understand sarcasm and Mr Zaccari sounds like a jerk.

'Maria, do you think I could find something related to law?'

'Don't you think that might be awkward for him, given that he's about to leave his practice?'

'That's true, poor man.'

It's no good, this Angela woman is clearly devoted to her boss.

'Is he married?'

'A widower, with three sons and a beautiful house.'

'OK, so what is his house like?'

'I don't know, I've never been inside… but he says it's beautiful, full of antique furniture.'

'Does he like travelling?'

'I think not, given that his motto is: A day off—'

'… yes, you said. Does he cook?'

'I know that the lady who comes in to clean cooks his meals, too.'

'Well, why don't you tell me a bit about him… off the top of your head.'

'Mr Zaccari is a great lawyer, you know? He's a role model, exceptional in his field. He could sway any jury, he's a strategist through and through. And he's handsome, despite his age, but I hope you won't misunderstand me.'

'Of course I won't, don't worry.'

I'd say it's pretty clear. This Angela woman is in love with the lawyer and would love to be the one living in the beautiful house.

'Angela, you haven't given me much to work on, to tell the truth… but let's see what we can do. Would it suit you to come back on Wednesday, when I'll have a few suggestions ready? Maybe in your lunch break. Unless you have to go home to your husband and kids…'

'No, no, I'm on my own.'

So I guessed correctly. The woman standing in front of me is an aspiring Mrs Zaccari.

'Perfect. I'll see you on Wednesday at 1 p.m., then. Angela? What about you? Do you have any hobbies?'

'Oh yes! I go to book club once a month and I play draughts, chess and bridge. I take part in buraco competitions, too.'

Enough with the buraco, it's an epidemic.

'That's great. I'll see you soon then.'

'See you on Wednesday.'

And she turned and headed straight towards the door of my shop, clutching her bag in both hands at knee height. All of a sudden, she looked back and said, 'Don't get me wrong, will you, I work a lot myself too.'

'Of course, I can see that.'

And out she went, the bell on the door jingling as she left.

My job is to find the right gift for the right person.

My clients can be divided into two types:

1) People who are more insecure than they are imaginative
2) People who are lazier than they are caring

Angela belongs to the first type. Many women find themselves in the first category.

The second group, the lazy uncaring ones, are mostly men, who claim something as theirs as soon as they've laid hands on it. Slow down, guys, you just set foot on the moon and planted a flag. That doesn't mean you can call it home.

Anyway, when I'm in a Mr Zaccari-type bind, my job is deadly boring. In fact, the job invariably resembles the person receiving the gift, and in this case, he's dry as dust.

And so my job can be miserable, daring, tall, blonde, brilliant, or quite disagreeable.

It's a question of matching like to like, and I have to be adaptable.

In short, when I'm saddled with the kind of person Angela is buying for, I just don't want to do it. I postpone and procrastinate, to the point that today is technically already Wednesday and I haven't come up with a single idea. Or rather, I hadn't until this auction that, at four in the morning, all-hallowed eBay proposes I join.

We all know what this old codger's retirement party will be like: a couple of fountain pens, maybe a watch from wealthier colleagues (or from those who want to look wealthy), a keychain, a picture frame, stuff like that. And then the inevitable bottle of expensive booze and/or a box of cigars. These events seem to be designed to instigate a heart attack rather than a rest.

By contrast, our Angela will be daring. Our Angela is going to give Mr Zaccari a piece of furniture. I can't wait to see her face when I suggest it. I hope I'll manage to convince her. I hope I'll still be convinced I made the right choice tomorrow, which is actually already today.

Maybe I'm so sleepy I'm making the wrong decisions.

To tell the truth, I don't really know whether I'm sleepy. But I do know that I'm tired.

I've skipped all my primary needs this shitty night. Like when you don't eat for a long time and you're no longer hungry. Or when you don't make love for a long time and you're no longer in love.

Like a sneeze that doesn't come.

As Nicola's back rises and falls in a steady rhythm, I lie next to him and try to sync up with him.

But he's breathing too fast and at his speed I can't breathe at all.

Ruth and I always went to bed at dawn in London, as the sky was turning pink. And when I say always, I mean every single night, even when there was no need.

We had to check. We had to be sure that the sun would rise.

Never trust what you know, Ruth would say.

And I'd say that is a better motto than Mr Zaccari's.

We would hang out and chat outside a club or a twenty-four-hour supermarket, or whisper in our room. Then, as we grew to know one another better, we managed to stay awake without talking.

When the dawn light arrived, our mission was accomplished: there was still life and we were witnesses to the fact. She calmed down and we were able to fall asleep in the arms of a new day.

She was obsessed, Ruth, with the fear that things would come to an end.

And I was jealous of her, of her inexplicable attachment to life.

I turn my back on Nicola and follow my own rhythm.

Pastime

Don't wake winter up
it hibernates in the summer
how strange

After Summer died, my parents were emaciated. My mother's face was drawn and her collarbone stuck out, making a furrow under her neck that fascinated me.

One afternoon, I came home from school, which I'd gone back to in time for my end-of-term report, and I needed to eat.

At the age of seven, my cooking skills were the same as they are now: non-existent. I've been a fan of raw food since long before it became a fad.

My mother was sitting at the table smoking, surrounded by balls of wool. My father was watching a film, staring into space.

I opened the fridge, grabbed a cup, poured some milk into it and burst open the wrapper of a cereal bar. The sound made my mother whip around, and that was when she saw me. She saw me!

She saw me so vividly she did her snap thing.

She'd started taking photos with her eyes again, I was sure of it.

'Mamma?'

'Yes, apricot. What is it?'

'Can I have breakfast for supper?'

'Whatever you want.'

So we had a bowl of cereal together. And from that moment on, she started talking to me again, actually talking.

Every time she talked to me, she said it wasn't my fault.

You know that, don't you?

Then she started sending me to the first psychologist who, every week, told me that it wasn't my fault. You know, don't you, that it's not your fault?

I would nod to keep them happy but I couldn't understand what they were so worried about. After all, I'd lived four years of my life on my own before Summer came along.

My sister wasn't like me, Mamma, Papà, our house, our two Maria grandmothers, the swing, the Pimpa video tapes. My sister hadn't been there forever. So it seemed logical to me that life without her would be possible.

I know, Mà, I know, doctor, it wasn't my fault.

In the meantime, my father had stopped going to work. He stayed home all day with the TV on.

My mother told me that he would be working in the living room from now on.

That was when the fax machine came into our lives, which soon became a trusted family friend, and by means of which my father managed to communicate, in faded print, with the world.

For many months, my father didn't take a shower, and the little hair he had stuck out of his head at random.

He no longer picked me up into his arms, and my mother said I should be happy because it meant my wish that I could grow up quickly had come true.

My mother would buy packets of wet wipes that my father cleaned his head and body with. She'd also come up with a cunning plan for the winter that was closing in annoyingly slowly that year, according to which she would stick the wipes in the microwave before handing them over to my father.

I didn't like having showers either, but my mother said I couldn't use the wipes. She said I could soak in the bath for as long as I liked, until I got old lady's fingers, white and crinkly.

I told all this to Ruth, years and years later, my accent like a mafioso's straight off the boat in America. But she understood everything, and she hugged me a lot on those interminable nights we spent waiting for the sun to rise.

I told her how vividly I remembered the pungent odour of my father's sweat at the time and the smell of that spring day when the men in white gloves took my sister away.

Death stinks, my friend. That's what I said to her.

She told me about her Aunt Lianne, who had taught her to draw up birth charts before she died of uterine cancer. And she said, yes, in her view too, death stinks.

'Of course it stinks. That way you create a bad memory and become more attached to life,' she said.

'But that would mean death has a purpose, when you always claim that pain has no purpose at all.'

'No, Mary. What I'm saying is that pain tells us that suffering sucks. It's the same with death, which stinks and therefore sucks.'

'OK. I get it. So, people should stop filling churches with sweet-smelling flowers at funerals.'

'Idiot.'

'*Stronza*.'

We would laugh and yell Italian swear words, which were the only words Ruth could say in my language because they were the only ones that I'd taught her.

'Talking about smells, have you had a shower today, *puttanna*?'

'How many times do I have to tell you? It's *puttana*, with only one N!'

We laughed out loud, our teeth white in the night.

When I met Ruth, with her long hair and ears full of piercings, I started to feel that it would have been nice to have had a sister, and that I didn't want to go home.

Ruth said she would stay with me for as long as she could. But that then she would have to return to Florida, because she was going back to college and she couldn't give up after all the money her parents had lent her to pay off her student loans.

'Ruth, are you good at swimming?'

'Are you kidding me? I'm great. I even won a few competitions.'

'What's your stroke?'

'Backstroke. You?'

'Freestyle is my thing. My backstroke isn't good.'

'Why not? It's beautiful!'

'Because when I go backwards I can't swim straight.'

'But you don't need eyes to swim, Mary.'

Here at home, our home, with Nicola that is, we don't have a bath in which to soak nasty thoughts away.

We have very practical solutions here because Nicola is the kind of practical guy who chooses an apartment based on the fact that the bathroom has black tiles and satisfactory water pressure.

I wonder how you can drown your sorrows without a bathtub.

Maybe when Nicola decided he liked the tiles, he still didn't know about sorrows. When I met him that evening at the bar with the grappa, I could see straight away that his colours had not been muddied yet.

Then, when they were, I saw his clumsy attempt to clean them, how anxious he was to bleach out the murky shades and return to the clear ones.

Many men take up with younger women, not just for the sex, which is theoretically more generous, but also to be able to form them. To have a blank slate on which to write their story, dictate their taste in restaurants, their circle of shared friends.

I felt the same potential when I met Nicola with his empty canvas standing on the easel, all the colours still in their pots.

I can't draw.

But it seems it's not necessary in contemporary art. All you need to do with a canvas, to make a work of art, is slash it.

Forget-me-not

I look for flowers with an odd number of petals
So I start with *he loves me* and end the same

Ruth and I exchanged addresses.

We wanted to lend weight to the words we would send one another by writing letters by hand, like in the old days. Giving our sentences the space to silt up a new strip of land that would reduce the distance from one side of the Atlantic to the other.

Because, I wonder if you knew this, Ruth? Seabeds can one day become mountains.

Our idea was a little romantic, destined to fail before we started, we knew it. And in fact, yes, we did send a few letters between her college and the hostel we once shared, but most of the time we filled the gaps with video calls and chats.

Not long after, I decided to go back to my parents' house, since by then I'd gone through my savings and London no longer seemed such fun.

Because in the meantime I'd started buying food at the supermarket, rather than cadging lunches at the Buddhist temple, as Ruth and I used to do. I'd stopped reading the palms of passers-by because, without her birth charts in front of me, I wasn't brave enough to lie.

Ruth read people well, she knew how to unlace them, unbutton them, without making a great to-do about it. It wasn't just their palm lines she interpreted. She also read their fingers, eyes, whether their shoulders were hunched, the way they walked and sometimes even their internal organs.

I used to think I understood other people's lives.

But she understood people better. Her desire not to be hypnotic made her all the more so. All she had to do was tuck her hair back from her forehead with a tinkle of her bracelets and she had the whole universe at her feet. She smoked slowly, and curled her legs up under her, whatever chair she was sitting on.

One day, while we were pretending to meditate at the Buddhist temple so we could get into the canteen, she told me in a whisper that she'd had a great idea.

'Do you realise how much trash there is in the world? Heaps and heaps of disgusting objects fuelling people's disgusting tastes? Have you seen the shit people give their kids, those fake machine guns and dolls with the terrifying eyes? We're so used to seeing this plastic crap everywhere that we don't even notice it any more.

'Mary, let's become gift-buying consultants! We'll have a shop with nothing on sale, no shelves, just brilliant ideas.

'We'll nourish beauty and imagination, my friend. We'll educate people, Mary. Educate them on how to give. *Be Present!* as they say here at the temple. Actually, that's a pretty awesome name for a shop that teaches you how to give presents.'

Ruth often had awesome ideas. Who knows what else she would come up with once she left college?

After I walked her to the Tube station, the day she left London, I didn't feel like doing anything. I felt heavy.

I was spending far more time in the hostel and found myself wandering the same streets day after day.

I'd turned into a tourist with nothing left to see.

Capstone

Bridging peaks
with vertigo, wind and rope

The only good thing about Ruth leaving was that I could go back to sleeping at night, but I realised it wasn't easy to get back into the habit.

I would stare at a fixed spot and softly sing nursery rhymes to myself.

Twinkle, twinkle, little star...

It didn't work.

A bit like this long, long night ten years later: nothing is working.

One night I slipped a sweatshirt over my pyjamas and went to see Adri, a Spanish guy we'd met when he served us coffee at Pret, who Ruth would fuck every now and again.

He was always very calm, extremely slow in his movements, with strong supple arms that undulated symmetrically as he wove between the tables.

His shoulders were at just the right height, like Ruth's but not like mine, which are so tense and hunched it's as though they're magnetically attracted to the sky or the ceiling of whatever room I'm in.

I wanted to try him out myself, that night.

Then we got dressed and sat there in silence, hypnotised by the lit-up sign of Holloway Road station outside the window. Until finally a brighter light came and we fell asleep back-to-back, as if a line had been drawn down the middle of the bed.

Dear Ruth, Last night, I went to bed with Adri and I didn't like it. Also, I've decided to go back home to Italy.

My lovely Mary, sex with Adri is good sex for sewing yourself together again.

It's not right for you, because you're all of a piece. Send new address for letters, please.

Tightrope

I tie a thread to my boots
and to your silver bracelets
they keep step
with their tinkling

I't's 5 a.m.

In exactly twelve hours, I have a doctor's appointment, and in exactly half an hour, Nicola's alarms are going to start going off, one after the other.

Can a person die from too little sleep? Or sooner or later do we collapse in order to save ourselves?

Do we let ourselves explode or are we programmed to shut down, like an overheated electronic device?

On my last day in London, it was pouring with rain and I went out to catch the bus that would take me to the Tube that would take me to the train that would take me to the shuttle bus that would finally take me to the aeroplane, like a treasure hunt with no treasure at the end.

The drops weren't the usual soft, persistent little needles. For the first time in those twelve weeks that felt more like twelve years, it actually rained. The kind of rain that from the hostel to the bus stop soaked me to the skin from my hair to my socks.

I tried covering my rucksack with my jacket and sheltering under the few balconies I came across.

I wondered: can a person rust to death?

If I stay this wet, will I go rusty and stop working?

Like the cogs in an antique clock.

And can a person die of time? My father might manage. It's different to dying of old age. Dying of time means just waiting, it means dying of dust. It means dying of patience, it means being eroded, slowly, by the wind.

The wind is a game changer.

Stone, paper, scissors. That game teaches us that you win some and you lose some. Nothing can be certain as long as an enveloping hand can destroy a stone.

That's what the wind does, slowly, never showing off its strength.

There are lives that let themselves get worn down. It's not even certain that every step will leave a footprint.

That was what I was thinking as I turned to rust on my way home.

Forecast

Cyclic depression from the north
will bring uncertain weather
to most of the area

Both of my parents made sure they were at the airport, actually inside, on the other side of the metal bar that separates those who are being waited for from those who are waiting.

My mother was smiling like crazy and waving her hand in case I couldn't see her, even though we were looking each other in the eyes by that point. Even my father looked happy.

On our way home, we stopped and had a pizza while I told them about my journey and responded, with a few omissions, to their cross-interrogation. I dwelt on the things they wanted to hear, like the fact that I'd made a good friend called Ruth and that, yes, I'd stayed a bit longer than planned but the result was that I'd been able to get a better grasp of the language.

'Did you do any of your university work?'

With my Roman History textbook, one evening, we killed a spider. That was it.

'A little.'

'Are you all set to go back?'

'While I was in London, I had an idea. I'd like to set something up on my own. A business.'

'What about university?'

'I'd do that at the same time, but I've had this really original idea and I think it could work. I don't want to waste any more time.'

That was how, as I scrounged the burnt edges of pizza off my parents' plates, I told them that I wanted to open a shop that wasn't really a shop, but rather a sort of studio where people could come and choose the perfect present for someone. And I would find it, Mà, and I would lighten the load of people's thoughts, Pà, and enrich them at the same time. By eliminating some of the ugliness from this world, some of the fondue sets, candles and bubble bath, all the presents given in haste and out of duty.

'That's wonderful, darling.'

'Interesting, Maria,' my father said.

'And yet, when you were a child, you didn't want any presents. Do you remember, apricot? You used to give presents without wanting any in exchange. You've always been so generous.'

I remembered all right.

And I also remember the relief when the Christmas charity raffle came around, which was when I could get rid of all my possessions.

Even now, with Nicola, I hate the fact that he'll start a new bottle of shampoo, a new packet of biscuits, a new kitchen roll, without throwing the old one away. He always leaves a drop, a crumb, a shred, something to justify keeping what was there before.

I hate this complex of his, this inability to finish things.

My mother was right that I didn't want any presents when I was little. But in the end, they bought them for me anyway. And receiving them was excruciating.

Once there was an advert on the telly for Mermaid Barbie and I committed the imprudence of saying that I thought she was beautiful, with her tail that shimmered like butterfly wings and Easter egg foil. A few months later, as I ripped the package open under the Christmas tree, I watched her blonde hair full of shells slowly emerge.

Like when the mist fades on the mirror as you dry your hair after a shower. And you watch yourself reappear in front of your own eyes with a shiver of apprehension.

When I saw the doll, I wanted to cry. I didn't cry. I never played with her. She was happy in her box.

The hidden surprises in Easter eggs, on the other hand, are incidental gifts: unpretentious, small, unknowable in advance. Nobody is ever surprised to find them again later in the raffle.

'Mà, what are you talking about? Everybody likes presents.'

'You're right. Hey, love, leave the edges. Don't you know it's bad for you to eat burnt stuff? You need to finish your own pizza. You're letting the best bits get cold.'

Killjoy

If you can't lie
you can't love

Dear Mary Maria,
  Ready for lots of questions?
  How was the journey? Ready for college?
  Do you miss London? Do you miss me?
  Friendship test: if I had parsley in my teeth, would you tell me?

Dear Ruth, Ruta, yes.
  Answers: Fine. Not really. Yes. Yes. Of course.
  Counter-test: if I wanted to pluck my eyebrows to look like seagull wings, would you lock my hands up in chains to stop me?

She would, she answered. And she told me about her cousins, Aunt Lianne's kids, with whom she wanted to come to Italy to see me the following summer.

I wrote that I didn't expect her to be such a long-term planner, and that she would win everyone's hearts here with her happy-go-lucky temperament and her fortune-telling skills.

I wish I were as smart as you, Maria. I wish I were as clear-headed.

I've met this amazing man, who's clearly problematic, but I can't get him out of my head. He has a sixteen-year-old daughter (which shows he's not exactly a spring chicken) and he's a gynaecologist (please let's not make predictable jokes about this).

His skin is the same colour as Adri's. He could be his father! LOL.

His birth chart is amazing and his moustache is quite ridiculous.

I answered this letter in a text, since I needed to keep it short and sweet.

She wished she were like me? I would never have expected this from her. Also, Ruth in love with a real doctor? A chiropractor, sure. A DJ or a pirate.

She was always one step ahead of any prediction that could be made about her.

It was typical of her to make even normality seem crazy, to make a man who was in the middle of a clichéd midlife crisis look as though he was speeding down a one-way road in the wrong direction.

My father liked the idea of the shop. I didn't expect that, either.

To me it sounded like something New Age, something that only made sense when discussed in a Buddhist temple on the River Thames.

He started telling people about it. Not faxing or emailing about it. He talked about it using his voice. I heard him telling my grandmother about it, talking it over with my mother in their bedroom, discussing it with his buraco friends. Everybody thought it was an incredibly good idea.

'What were you doing in London all this time, Maria?' people would ask me.

I lived like billions of other human beings who live and think they are doing something but aren't really doing anything, while the universe goes on expanding and we go on shrinking, I wanted to yell.

'I did some research for a start-up,' is what I would say instead.

'Oh, wow.'

That was how from a quiet country lane I found myself veering onto a slick motorway where I could slip and slide at speed without ever changing gear.

Nonna Maria, the necklace grandmother, lent me the money to get started.

I'd found a place in the town centre, a small place because that's what I needed.

I'd found an awesome name.

I'd found the lighting and furnishings.

I'd even thought about the invitation design for the launch.

Dear Ruth,

I finally did that bloody Roman History exam, that heavy tome I was reading in London. I got 30 cum laude, *which would be equivalent to an A+.*

But I think I've had enough of university.

How are things with Mr Moustache?

Baby Mary, you're such a nerd.

I'm going crazy. I can't concentrate on my studies because I keep thinking about Mark (Mr Moustache! LOL).

How many hours are there in an hour without Mark? And without you?

Maybe I'll ask him to come with me and my cousins to visit you.

I feel like this winter is going to be really long. An ocean is too great a distance.

What do you want to do once you give up university? A trip around the world?

Dear Ru, I'll come up with something.

Anyway, I've always thought Adri was madly in love with you.

Maybe you should have got together.

In the meantime, the preparations were going ahead.

My twenty-fourth birthday came and – quickly, thankfully – went.

I decided to open the shop on 15 December, in time for potential Christmas clients.

Ruth posted me a photo of her with Mr Moustache, one of those kitsch American cards saying *Happy Xmas* with snowflakes Photoshopped on top. They were smiling at one another from different but matching armchairs that faced each other. It looked like an ad for low-cholesterol cheese.

It pissed me off: her legs curled up on the chair and her stupid long hair and her white teeth and little fur boots and that need to jingle her earrings and bracelets whenever she came into a room so as not to go unnoticed.

That Christmas card made her look so horrendously normal.

I answered with this:

You need to know what to wish for before it can come true.
*You are invited to the inauguration of **BePresent!***
15 December at 6 p.m. at via Garibaldi 21

At the launch, there were lots of people who were curious to suss out the strange little place. I explained it to everyone, more and more enthusiastically as I glugged more and more Prosecco.

And that was how I ended up drunk on the idea that I was engaged in a business venture, as serious people would call it, a shop into which I, if I were ever in my customers' place, would never set foot but which almost immediately became trendy.

I'd locked my own hands up in chains.

Just as much then as now, when yet another day in that hole of a place awaits me. I was surrounding myself with people like Mr Zaccari and Angela, people who are insecure, unhappy, boring and lazy.

I got down to work immediately and worked hard, sourcing Rollerblades for accountants, harmonicas for sad people, poems written but not signed by me for extramarital lovers, day trips to farms for kids, copies of Seneca's *On the Shortness of Life* for anyone and everyone, like confetti.

Over time, I realised that the key was nostalgia: seeking memories and reliving them.

Memories of childhood.

I started to realise that people are moved by stories, addicted to context.

So I rummaged through flea markets, online auctions, classified ads.

It was the beginning of my career as Cyrano, with a slightly better nose.

Halfway through January, as I arrived for lunch at my parents' house, which at the time was my house too, I found a letter in the postbox.

In the envelope was a card with only one word written on it:

Puttanna

PART TWO

Breakfast

Stronghold

Can't you see there's no difference
between the wall of a fortress
and the wall of your room
if the war is waging inside?

*R*_{*ing*}.

Fuck…

Ring.

I swear I'd just closed my eyes.

Ring.

Horrific timing.

Ring.

'Good morning, my love.'

'Morning,' I say.

He curls up against me, grabbing me with his arm, which is boiling hot, the temperature of somebody who has slept straight through the night.

I feel terribly sleepy, the heat makes me feel sleepy.

That's why I don't like going to the beach. When I go, I strip, jump in, swim, get out and that's that, *ciao*. Otherwise I end up not wanting to do anything.

He winds his leg around mine, I can't hold off any longer, I give in to sleep.

Nicola and I are in a room that is completely white, like a doctor's surgery or a lab in a science fiction film.

'My feet are hurting, Maria. Help, they hurt. My eyes are hurting, Maria. I beg you, do something, Maria! Maria! My head, too! Ow! Ow! My whole head, Maria! My forehead hurts... my temples, too. Help me! Oh no! My hair!'

Calm down. Think.

'I can't. I can't think, Maria! It hurts too much. It's too much! I can't walk any more, I can't see, I can't think. Talk to me, Maria! Save me!'

Think, Nicola. Think. Your pain can be explained.

Your feet hurt because your shoes are too tight, see? Unlace them.

Your eyes hurt because you're wearing glasses but you don't need to wear them. Take them off.

Your head hurts because...

Ring.

Riiiing.

No, not again.

'Nicola, the alarm... is ringing... again.'

He gropes for it, silences it.

I want to go back to sleep to see how the dream ends. Why was his head hurting?

But duty calls, his, that is, because today he's off to Paris or Dublin, I can't remember which, just that he'll be back in time for dinner.

'How's your belly?'

'What?'

'Your belly was hurting last night, how is it today?'

'Oh, yes, it's still hurting.'

These are the petty answers to life's questions after the alarm has rung.

'Oh no, poor Mary Mine. Did you get any sleep?'

'A little, yes.'

'Thank goodness… maybe next month will be the one. We'll try again.'

The right month for him is the month my period fails to come.

He means we'll try again to have a baby.

He who gets up at dawn to fly.

I who feel relieved to stay on the ground.

Whatever

There's no blood, nor flight, nor violence
in my pain
there's only patience

And anyway, who would we give birth to, Nicola?

A mythological child, half-seagull, half-cat.

What if it took after me and learnt to swim fast?

Trying to be in too many realms makes you unsuited to any of them.

Whatever, Nicola, find me one human being who is totally suited to life and introduce me to them.

You'd say that we are, that we could be.

You, from the bottom of your love for form, for labels, would say that we'd be consummate parents. Exemplary.

You who believe you're immune to dirt.

I know you can't see, with your eyes that only hurt at night, that we're penguins, you and I.

We can walk and swim but we've been put in the wrong category. Formally, we're supposed to be able to do something that we can't in reality. We're only birds on our identity cards, Nicola.

This lovable lummox with tiny wings, so well dressed, so popular.

Do you know that male penguins hatch the eggs, not females? Yes, you know it, and you smile when you think about it.

Do you know, Nicola, that I walk barefoot on ice for miles and miles, every year, every day, every moment?

Can you tell me why last night your head was hurting in my dream? Please?

Maybe because you intercept my thoughts?

Do you know, Nicola, that what you do is not flying? You pilot a plane. You need to acknowledge it. You're a trucker, a rider, a driver nobody can talk to.

What the fuck do you know, Nicola, when you smile at me as soon as you wake up?

'What are you thinking about, Mary?'

'Nothing.'

Greenhouse

Rage didn't take me to war
just to the window

He must have asked me a thousand times in these seven years, 'What are you thinking about?'

I've often answered like I did just now, 'Nothing.'

And over time, he's managed not to investigate any further. The same person who dissects vegetables when he slices them, and who hangs his shirts straight so they're easier to iron, has surprisingly learnt to dig less.

But he reads my texts and emails, and checks my received calls.

I've known for a long time and I pretend not to know, who gives a fuck?

The first time he asked me was the first time we had sex, the evening we drank the grappa.

That's right, the evening we met at the bar. After a certain age, I say, what's the point of waiting to have sex with someone? You'll end up there anyway, right? You may as well get it over and done with.

I've never been afraid of looking easy to get. In fact, I would have quite liked it. But no, it's always been difficult.

Anyway, that evening after the bar we went to my shop and did what people do.

'What are you thinking about, Maria?'

'The months of the year. You?'

'About you. You're beautiful.'

'How can you be thinking about me if I'm right here?'

'Well... of course I'm thinking about you, precisely because you're here. Where do the months of the year come into it?'

Thirty days hath November, April, June and September.

That's what I was thinking.

I was thinking that there was one with twenty-eight and all the rest had thirty-one.

Other times we made love, I went through the first kings of Rome: Tullio Ostilio, Anco Marzio, Numa Pompilio and the other four on the list.

Or simple prepositions, of from to in with on by through between, or Latin declensions, rosae rosarum rosis et cetera.

Not out of any lack of respect, mind you. Far from it.

I do it while I'm swimming, too, reciting poems I learnt off by heart at primary school, or the names I can recall on the intercom of my building, like Eleonora Marelli.

What else should I be thinking about?

About our naked bodies writhing? I can already see them.

Lifting my head out of the water in time to breathe? I already do that.

What if I were thinking about what I have to do tomorrow, about the scratch card for the parking meter that's about to expire, or about whether I forgot to turn the lights off when I went out? Now that would be rude.

Nursery rhymes are just harmless words, they numb you, they don't add content, just a lovely sound, to the silence that reigns underwater and to Nicola's little groans when he's making love, when he's concentrating on form even at that moment, taking care not to explode, ever.

'But Nicola… you can't only think about the things you can see. I mean, imagine what a disaster it would be if, when the apple fell on his head, Newton had thought about how delicious apples were!'

'Well, you're actually beautiful. But I was thinking, too… that I hope there's a bathroom in this place… we've had a lot of beer and I'm bursting!'

We both laughed. He, in spurts, as always, with that gap in the middle that sucked my own voice into the air pocket.

Then, naked and pretty unclean, we held each other tight on the uncomfortable armchair in the shop. So precarious that we couldn't move an inch, so tight that, for the first time, I collapsed into his warm body, as if it were a new womb.

I woke up the next morning as the slightly raised shutter cut a ray of sun into slices.

We had been completely still, like flesh statues.

The walls were sparkling with dawn light.

The colour of the room made me think of freshly squeezed orange juice, which reminds me of winter, which reassures me.

While petting the night before, he told me he was a pilot and that we were more or less the same age. And yet we'd never crossed paths.

Or maybe we had, but we didn't notice one another, we'd filtered each other out as irrelevant information, until that moment.

We'd discovered we had a few friends in common and a deep-rooted but not drastic hatred for the city we lived in. Which he had exorcised by becoming a pilot and I had by knitting boredom into sweaters that I could wear.

At that moment, when I looked at him, still nude, perched on my armchair, he seemed perfect for the role of mouse or guinea pig, ready for a lab test.

How did those long legs manage to fold up so well?

He looked small and heavy, compact, as if he could increase his unit weight by concentrating his entire being into one spot.

You need to be light to be able to fly.

And yet aeroplanes, people, baggage, engines, fuel, meal trolleys are all heavy.

So, unless you're a hopeless penguin, you can achieve flight in one of two ways:

1) You have natural talent, like the balloon I freed into the sky years ago
2) You're a hard worker and you keep trying, calculating and trying again, until you find the solution

That's what Nicola was: an artificial solution, masterfully put together.

Lifejacket

I clasp you with nettle hands, my spirit,
and squeeze and squeeze

I turn the gas on under the coffee pot and go to the bathroom to brush my teeth.

I know you're not supposed to do it, that it's sacrilegious to brush your teeth before drinking coffee, but I can't start the day in this state, my mouth furry with dreams from the night before.

And yet I go back to them and whenever I manage to remember a dream I tell it to myself over and over the next morning to keep it from going away.

Brushing each tooth one by one, from top to bottom, I go over the scenes of my father and the rainbow and the deserted beach and the world collapsing on top of me. Of Nicola with all that pain that was easy for me to explain but not for him. Considering he really does suffer from physical pain.

Everything is always aching, especially his back. He blames runway landings, strain, invisible whips that crack against him.

I don't know how he manages. Personally, I think when people say 'it's all about the journey, not the destination', it's the biggest lie ever.

Nicola's life is this expression in a nutshell, the cliché bandied around at a fat ladies' book club: all he has is the journey and he never arrives anywhere.

Today he'll go to Paris or Dublin, but it's a lie. He'll go to Paris airport or Dublin airport, it doesn't make the slightest difference which, they're all the same, all grey. Airports are like my mother, they never know what side to sit on, they prefer not to expose themselves to chromatic choices, personalities, bright colours.

The true destination is the destination. And an airport is not that.

My father has also suffered a great deal, physically.

A year or so after I killed Summer, he went back to having showers but his legs started aching. He said they kept going to sleep and that it was hard to move them.

It made me laugh thinking of legs going to sleep on their own and, before going to bed at night, I would recite in my head, 'goodnight, hands, goodnight, nose, goodnight, legs, goodnight, papà, goodnight, everyone.'

I remember some days when my father stayed on the sofa all day, his legs numb, surrounded by open VHS cases, the fax machine spitting out messages for him from the newsroom.

My father, Peppe, has always been a sports and culture journalist for the local paper. Bari played well, or Bari would be relegated to the second division, exhibitions in town, jazz concerts as if anyone actually likes jazz, important events for the patron saint Nicola, where have all the funds earmarked for culture gone? I don't think that working from home changed his job much. I think that his job has always been to do as little as possible, to stay afloat, even when he used to go to the newsroom before that day twenty-five years ago.

He would type a few lines, copying here and there from press releases and articles in the national papers from the day before, he would interview a trainer or a painter on the phone. Then he'd put it all through the magic fax machine that would transport his words somewhere else.

'Papà, why do you put the paper in there?'

'So that it can travel to my colleagues.'

'But how can it travel if I can still see it here?'

'It's hard to explain.'

I wanted to try and fax myself, too, and I asked him if I could but he said it wasn't possible. Come on. It sounded like a really interesting experience, being teletransported without moving at all.

Come to think of it, it sounds exactly like what Nicola does when he goes to work.

Exactly like what my sister did that day when I saw her all blue in front of me, when in fact she was no longer there.

A few years later, emails were invented, which you could write on the computer but which needed a phone line. So the fax machine became an accessory, before being relegated to the division of 'garage junk'.

'Maria! Get off the phone! I'm working. Maria, put the phone down! There, damn it! You cut me off.'

I did it on purpose, lifting the receiver so I'd get told off.

Of course, every morning we bought the paper he wrote for, and I went straight to the back pages which carried the articles signed with my dad's initials, G. D. After his pieces, I flicked through to the horoscopes to see what was in store for Libra, my sign, and totally ignored the other eleven.

According to the paper, everything was always fine.

This was why my parents' house always smelt of ink and flowers: mountains of daily papers piled up in the sitting room and a bunch of freshly cut flowers every three days, always white, for their other daughter.

Summer never disconnected my parents, even though she left.

And I, who stayed behind, had been sent by my father somewhere else, like words in the fax machine.

Mine and Nicola's house, on the other hand, smells of coffee at all hours of the day.

Particularly right now as I run into the kitchen at the spluttering sound of the coffee pot. I turn off the gas.

Nicola is bracing the door of the living room-studio-bunker doing foot pumps. It's his morning stretching routine, designed to limit the damage to his back from flying.

Every morning, even when I get up at the crack of dawn, our kitchen table is laid like a five-star-hotel buffet. Breakfast is the only good thing about hotels and, in truth, the only meal worthy of note at all.

Primarily because you're allowed to drink coffee without being pestered about the caffeine. If I told Nicola that I didn't sleep a wink last night, he would begin to lecture me, with Cub Scout verve, on the supposed side effects of caffeine.

Look inside me, my love. Change the lens on your camera, ditch the close-up and zoom in deeper. Come in, Nicola, try to see beyond what's physically here.

Do you really believe I don't sleep because of the coffee?

He's always vigilant, always attentive, he notices immediately if I've cut my hair or moved a piece of furniture.

My mother and my friends tell me how lucky I am to have a man who notices the small things, the things their own partners don't see.

Ruth would never have said that.

She would have rolled a cigarette, her eyebrow raised (just one, her right), and wanted to know all about his childhood, his dreams, his birth chart, what sex positions he likes, in the light, in the dark.

Because a love affair is not a puzzle in the back of the newspaper.

Spot the twenty differences between these two images.

Bravo, Nicola, you found them all. I feel like I'm in a relationship with Jessica Fletcher.

But now, love, you have to tell me why.

Why did I cut my hair last week?

Why did I refurbish the shop last year?

But here, Mr Detective, you need more than just your eyes.

Goodnight, sight.

We're two strangers who have learnt each other by heart.

We know each other's moles, scars, gestures.

Two necklaces coiled together in a jewellery box that take time and nimble fingers to untangle.

Goodnight, touch.

We can even anticipate what the other is about to say, but that's statistics rather than telepathy.

Goodnight, hearing.

We're a TV ad for a perfume, artistic and conceptual, with a guest star and a slogan in French. Where there's everything but the fragrance, everything but what counts.

Goodnight, smell.

We're two strangers who one evening seven years ago, almost eight, drank a glass of grappa and this morning will drink a cup of coffee.

Goodnight, taste.

Goodnight, senses, goodnight, legs, goodnight, everybody.

Daybreak

We're shoelaces
tripping over ourselves

Coffee, cereal, oat milk, milk-milk, biscuits, fruit, bread, eggs, jam, yoghurt. Nicola sits down and drowns three teaspoons of sugar in his coffee cup. I decide not to pick a fight.

'Where are you going today? Paris?'

'No, no. Don't you remember?'

'Ah, yes. Dublin.'

'No, Dublin is the day after tomorrow. Today it's Milan. Twice.'

'Bari-Milan-Bari-Milan-Bari?'

'Yes.'

'Fun.'

'Really.'

He laughs, but it's just for form's sake, hunching his shoulders with no trace of the hole in the middle.

'Listen, since I'm coming back halfway through the day, if you want we could grab a coffee at the airport this afternoon. What do you say?'

'No, I can't. I'm busy today.'

'At the shop, or somewhere else?'

'The shop.'

He knows I'm lying.

But he can't show it without giving himself away, without admitting that he's keeping tabs on my phone and the rest of it.

That's why I wrote DOCTOR on my Google calendar, today at 5 p.m.

To make him read it and go crazy with questions.

That's also why I list my clients by their initials, so he never knows whether they're men or women, to keep him constantly on edge.

Today, on my calendar, I have, for example A. x Z., 1 p.m., which means 'Angela for Zaccari' and I know full well that these letters in his head stand for men, always men, maybe with backs that ache a little less than his.

'I'll see you tonight then.'

'Yes.'

'What would you like for dinner?'

A life spent planning meals.

Sitting at breakfast thinking about dinner: this is what grown-up life is like.

Before moving in with Nicola, I never thought about dinners. Meals appeared in my life thanks to my grandmothers, thanks to my father, thanks to my mother, whose cooking has always been disastrous, thanks to Adri who brought us leftovers from the bar in his attempts to conquer Ruth.

How am I supposed to know now what I'd like to have this evening?

'We could go out for a pizza or a Chinese?'

That's how I answer him, calmly, to stifle any further inner controversy and not let it spill out.

'OK, I'm in! But I'll be home late.'

'That's fine, we'll go late.'

'Maria, is there something to celebrate by any chance?'

'I don't think so.'

'OK, pizza it is.'

I put another pot of coffee on.

Nonplussed

Because, basically,
you always know everything

For exactly a year, Nicola's been spying on me.

And for exactly a year he's been terrified of being found out. But, as I've already said, I know and I have no intention of extracting any confessions.

It all started a couple of years ago, when Nicola's father had pancreatic cancer. That is, since Nicola's father found out he was going to die.

For the first five years, life as a couple was great for me.

For six days in a row, he was never home and only came back at night to help me sleep, his body radiating heat.

He would then have five days off, when he slept a lot, took care of domestic stuff and proposed day trips, which I occasionally accepted on weekends. Then he would go again, and come again. The waves kept saturation at bay.

His shifts haven't changed, but now it's sort of as if he is always here, rifling through my head.

We moved into this apartment immediately after we met, with the haste of accomplices in a crime who leave the car engine on, no time to think, with the speed of people who need to survive and so run.

Me, from a house that was too empty, him from one that was too full.

The house Nicola grew up in is a bazaar stuffed with knick-knacks kept from weddings over the years and children's mouths to feed. Five in total. He, the firstborn, followed by four girls. Every part in its right place.

Nicola did his best to live up to the aspirations of his old-school father.

Meaning, basically, that he didn't believe a girl would ever provide any kind of intellectual or social satisfaction for her parents except for finding an eligible bachelor and, thus, procreating.

I never liked Nicola's father, because he was old-school and because of the way he stuck his elbows squarely on the table when he sat at its head.

Nicola, however, venerated him.

He called him practically every evening to talk, ritualistically and almost monosyllabically, about men's stuff.

'All good at work, Papà?'

'Of course. You?'

'All good.'

'And the raise? Are you getting the raise?'

'Maybe next year.'

'You need to demand things, boy. Demand them. Do you think they'll just give them to you?'

'No.'

'If I hadn't demanded things, I would never have got to where I am now.'

'I know, Papà.'

'I'll pass you your mother.'

And that was where the ritual called for the languid Ada to step in.

Despite her languor, I really like her: so much for the historic rivalry between mother and daughter-in-law.

The fact is, there has never been any rivalry between us. I've never been in a position to give advice on how to get a stain out of my boyfriend's shirt, I've never had a recipe that I didn't find on the internet, I've never dared sew a hem on a pair of curtains.

The fact is that Nicola can do everything on his own. Precisely because he spent many years as a child with his housewife mother and four sisters.

Because he spent hours playing at baking cakes, pairing up socks and drying tomatoes on the balcony, while their father, only metaphorically, brought the bread to the table running his haulage company, Regina Bros.

Whose brothers they are I don't know, since Nicola's dad only had sisters, too, and obviously they couldn't be his partners. Maybe it was just his way of turning himself into a plural noun and feeling strength in numbers, or perhaps it was just one more of the brilliant ideas of this visionary southern Italian entrepreneur.

I've always had a cordial relationship with Nicola's mum, Ada, for the simple reason that I've never competed with her.

I've never wanted Nicola to love me more than he loves her.

With his sisters, too, things have always gone well precisely because I've never examined them closely enough to distinguish one from the other. They've always pitied me, a murderer unable to be a real woman, with the atypical accessory of a shop in her name.

I could live with Nicola in the same house but I couldn't steal his heart.

And yet I did, but it wasn't my fault.

I hadn't stolen his heart, I'd simply found it in my bag and didn't know what to do with it.

So I buried it in the garden, still pulsing and covered in blood, but I forgot to leave a mark or a stone on the ground to be able to find the spot again.

I wanted to give him his heart back, but I didn't know where to dig for it.

The clumps of grass all look the same, like my sisters-in-law.

Masterpiece

... the missing tile

One July evening, two years ago, Nicola's languid mother called with the news.

Pancreatic cancer. Metatheses in the liver and lungs and who knows where else?

They'd known for a month already and they hadn't told Nicola yet, he was the only one in the dark.

Everyone else knew, even the four Siamese sisters.

The only one they hadn't told was Nicola because, as they said, they didn't want to upset him. They didn't want him to lose focus at work, at least until they knew how the treatment was going and what the outlook was.

Outlook?

The languid Ada sobbed, theatrically but sincerely, I think.

'Mamma, I'm coming right away.'

And there it was: after all those blinding colours, the first dark stain in his life.

Nicola's family, like a bas-relief at the bottom of a church door depicting the netherworld, lives in a town thirty-five kilometres from ours, which to them feels like an eight-hour time difference, or the other side of the wardrobe in Narnia, or a Stargate with a balcony looking out over another dimension.

'Maria.'

'Nicola, what do you want me to do?'

'Maria.'

'Tell me.'

'Come with me, I beg you, come with me.'

We went. I drove.

My thighs stuck to the car seats it was so hot, even though it was nearly dark.

Unusually, he wasn't saying anything and I didn't interrupt the miracle, of course. It didn't feel right to turn the radio on, it was time for silence. The only exception was the air coming through the window that made a noise, the blissful sound of freedom.

I recited in my head Mary Mary quite contrary how does your garden grow.

Nicola wound the window up. Goodnight, air.

He was staring straight ahead at the road, more vigilant than me, even though I'd been assigned the driving. He looked down at the gearbox whenever I needed to change, as if he were driving telepathically.

He followed the curve with his head, as a motorcyclist would, or as Antongiulio would if he were a real dog, and when I overtook, he craned his neck to make sure that everything was OK in the other lane.

We got there. I switched the engine off.

I unfastened my seat belt to encourage him to do the same.

He grabbed my hand.

'Maria.'

'What?'

'Don't leave me.'

'No, I'm here.'

'Maria.'

'Hey.'

'Don't leave me, ever.'

I smiled, we got out of the car and rang the intercom.

Where had I put this heart? Where the fuck did I bury it? A metal detector wouldn't work for this, would it?

Why didn't I cover it in coins so that it would beep?

Why didn't I drive a nail in to mark the spot?

Why didn't I think of drawing a map with a giant X on it?

At least a headstone, like Summer's, which says, *We will love you forever, little angel.*

The languid mother opened the door wearing a sleeveless dress, the skin on her arms quivering, and flip-flops.

I wanted to disappear, I wanted to hand over the map: here, Ada, your firstborn's heart is right here, it's still pumping, go and get it, rinse the earth off and put it back in the chest it belongs to. I need to go. *Ciao.*

Instead, I closed the door behind me. I was inside.

I felt like an idiot, like someone who goes into a bridal shop with a chocolate ice cream in her hand, the tragedy in plain sight, the stain that will ruin everything, long before disaster strikes. It's not a matter of prescience, there are no superpowers involved, just common sense, just statistics, just the wisdom you gain when you habitually listen to the weather forecast.

The sisters, who fly in formation like geese, were in the kitchen pretending to busy themselves around the table.

The father was in his usual place.

Head of the table, empty coffee cup, white singlet, diary, cigarette, elbows.

Nicola opened his arms. His father didn't. With the result that Nicola, who didn't know what to do with his hands after this aborted gesture, rested them on his head like someone who would like to be thinking but doesn't have an idea.

'Why are you wasting your time coming over here this evening? How's work, Nico?'

'Papà.'

'Are they giving you that raise or not? When you start doing intercontinentals you can take us all to America.'

'Papà.'

'Be a man, Nicola. Come on.'

'Papà.'

The record was stuck.

I've come to realise that when you look it in the eye, death reduces you to one word, no matter whether it's the blue face of a beautiful little girl or the ribbed singlet of a man with a hairy back.

Nicola could only say Papà, just as my mother that day could only say No.

You focus on a concept and you repeat it a thousand times, a bit like when the words in the nursery rhymes that I recite blur into mere sounds. And when this happens, you start magically spitting out little shards of ice to soothe the wound or cool the sweltering summer evenings, like this one, when Nicola understood that colour could bleed into his pristine white life.

We stayed for dinner.

The geese sisters honked at me, saying they would come and see me at the shop since they'd received so many invitations to parties that year they'd run out of ideas.

'Girls, you really don't need to come all that way, there's nothing to see in the shop. Send me an email with a little information about the people you need gifts for and I'll do the rest.'

'An email? No way! It'd be far quicker to come over to your shop.'

Jesus.

Nicola and his mother stayed in the kitchen.

I think she'd been crying the whole time, which I deduced from the fact that unnecessary water kept running from the taps at the kitchen sink, maybe to cover her sobs.

His father didn't abandon his position for one second, while right under his nose the coffee cup and ashtray were magically whisked away, the tablecloth was spread out, pork chops appeared, dirty dishes vanished and the limoncello was brought in. Life, other people's lives, took place around him, while he sat there in the middle of the room without lifting a finger as if he were at the heart of a labyrinth.

Later, Nicola and I finally found a way to escape from that overcrowded house, after saying goodbye to the Minotaur in a singlet and threading our way through walls of bushes that were taller than us.

Metastasis

This is what we do:
detach and migrate

On our way back home that July night, Nicola, unusually, still wasn't talking.

There was air coming in the window, finally cool enough to give me goosebumps.

We arrived home.

Synchronised with the sound of the handbrake being pulled up, Nicola broke his silence.

'Maria, will you marry me?'

'Let's go to bed now, my love, you need a good rest. Maybe you'd better not go to work tomorrow.'

But the next day he did go to Berlin, I think… or Dublin.

Basically, he went wherever he had to.

And so did his father, forty days later.

Things went downhill rapidly, as September began and the grapes were harvested.

At the funeral, he asked me again, whispering audibly while total strangers came up and kissed him on the cheek.

'Maria, will you marry me?'

'I don't think you're in your right mind at the moment.'

'What's your problem with marrying me?'

'What are you talking about?'

'My father just died.'

'Nicola, I know. Do you know? That's the question.'

'My father died and we're not getting married.'

'Yes, that sums it up.'

'You don't understand.'

'No, I don't understand. But now's not the time.'

'When will it be time?'

'I have no idea. Let's go and help your mother.'

'I need to go and pay the priest.'

He was a broken man, his hands glued to his head again, his heart buried in the garden, his beautiful eyes at the bottom of the sea, his voice lost in a flurry of leaves and all those anonymous kisses pasted on his face.

I watched him crumple in front of my eyes, as if he were signalling that the autumn would be shit. Which it was.

He was small. He was shrinking by the second, like the night we first met on that armchair. Looking at him, I felt like I could pick him up and carry him up the stairs without waking him, like a child who's fallen asleep in the car at night. But there was no need, we live on the ground floor.

The more he shrank, the more I expanded, as if the atoms of my body were being pinged into space, dancing molecules in search of a new domain.

A rarefied one.

The second pot of coffee is coming to the boil.

'Do you want some?'

'No, Mary, I'm well awake now.'

As if coffee is only for waking up. Not everything has to have a purpose.

'Ok, Nico. Are you off?'

'Yes, I'd better go. Shall we meet at home or at the pizza place?'

'At home, then we can go together.'

'OK. Have a nice day, Mary Mine. I'll get dressed and go.'

'See you tonight.'

'See you tonight.'

Rubber-stamp kiss.

Earthquake

We're a house of cards
on a dancing table

After Nicola's marriage proposal on the day of Mr Regina Senior's funeral, there were others, all of which I ducked.

He would load a gun with the proposal and fire it at me, with no warning, no mercy. I would throw myself on the ground, holding my ears to muffle the sound of the shot.

He was in pieces, but he thought he was fixed, working all day and grinding his teeth all night, walking so fast you'd think he knew where he was going, even though he was lost.

He asked me to marry him all the time, when he came in from work, on his days off, when he came to pick me up at the shop, on Sunday at breakfast.

'Will you marry me?'

'Nicola, do you realise you haven't stopped for a minute since your father died?'

'Will you marry me?'

'Nicola, you need to get more sleep, for fuck's sake.'

'Will you marry me?'

'...'

'Will you marry me?'

'We'll talk about it later.'

But we never got around to talking about it. Because Nicola said things without saying anything.

And I never even started looking for the words.

Since that day in the summer, he'd become pocket-sized, he was so well camouflaged against the background of the house, against the cushions, that I forgot he was home.

I couldn't stand him any longer.

'Will you marry me?'
  'First you need to get yourself out of this tunnel.'
  'What tunnel?'
  'You know.'
  'OK.'
  'Fine.'
  'Mary, I don't know how to.'
  'Me neither.'

I didn't know how to help him, everything about him got on my nerves: his closely trimmed beard, his uniform, his shaky voice, his good looks.

So I decided to get an expert in: amazed by myself, I called my mother.

'Mà, you need to come and talk to Nicola.'

'Of course, apricot. I'll come this afternoon.'

She bustled in like Mary Poppins, impeccable, professional, filled with a mission, proffering a tray of little pastries.

The three of us sat around the table.

'Anna, can I offer you anything to drink, some tea perhaps?'

'Nicola, tell me… how are you?'

Boom.

My mother's a genius sometimes. All he needed to hear was the question and the flood gates opened. Nicola cried, at regular intervals, in the same way he laughed, with a hole in the middle.

My mother kept one hand on his, almost as if she were tying him down to the table.

I hadn't been assigned a specific role in the scene.

Without a word, I stole a chocolate eclair from the tray and took a nibble out of it.

'I feel terrible, Anna, or maybe I don't. I can't tell any more.'

'It's normal. It's completely normal. You need to get it out of your system.'

'I feel so stupid, Anna. Forgive me.'

And there it was: the first time in history that Nicola used the intimate *tu* with my mother, on that day a year and a half ago, asking her forgiveness with his hand trapped under hers.

'Why are you saying sorry? Sorry for what?'

'I'm sorry because I'm sitting here crying about my father. I mean… you lost a daughter, Anna… and here I am getting worked up about something that was going to happen sooner or later, that was in the natural order of things. What do I know about what you went through? What do I know about grief?'

'Listen carefully, Nicola. There's no ranking for grief. Is that clear? Competing between levels of grief makes no sense, nobody wins. Everybody loses.'

The eclair was delicious, I wasn't expecting that.

Blackjack

I've learnt to count cards
one's missing

I clear the table in a hurry and carelessly pile the dishes up in the sink. I'm always hoping something will break, a saucer, a cup, one less thing to wash, one more thing to throw away. But this morning, like every morning, nothing has shattered.

Shampoo, rinse, conditioner, repeat, feet, legs, move upwards, rub hard.

I think I'll wear the same clothes as yesterday, it'll be quicker. I'm tired.

Jeans, white shirt, brown boots, wet hair because the sound of the hairdryer would put me straight to sleep.

In the hostel room with Ruth and me, there was a Spanish girl for a few days who fell asleep with a hairdryer blowing right next to her pillow.

She said she couldn't fall asleep without it.

I thought it was something of a miracle she was still alive so far away from home, or still alive in general.

I grab my bag, my health card, a banana, my mobile, my toothbrush and the printout of the table that I'll be suggesting Angela buy.

It's from the early nineteenth century and it seems crazy that there are objects so much older than me wandering around the world for decades or centuries without ever getting broken.

Maybe the secret to living a long happy life is being a table, or a piece of wood, or a tree, or before that, a seed, a fruit, or a flower, like in that children's song Summer and I used to love where in order to make anything, you needed a flower. A beautiful white flower.

I lift the roller door up.

In my shop there's a desk, two chairs and a lamp. That's all. It's like an interrogation room in an American TV series, but a bit more sophisticated. It's how I imagine an interrogation room in Sweden or Denmark might be.

I refurbished the place in this style last year, and put wallpaper on the walls that looks like a forest.

It sounds ugly when I describe it, but it's actually beautiful.

The bathroom door is camouflaged by the undergrowth, so fewer people ask me if they can use it.

I've created a habitat for myself. I'm like an animal in a safari park: I'm still in a cage, but I can assuage any guilt tourists may feel.

I sit on the ground, completely immersed in this fake but comforting natural setting, and wait.

At 9.30, I hear a knock.

'Buongiorno.'

'Hi, I don't have much time. I'll fill you in quickly.'

'Hi. I was expecting you at nine, in fact. Do sit down.'

'Busy time at work.'

'How can I help you?'

'I have to get my wife a present, I've heard you're good.'

'It depends. Tell me more.'

'…What can I say? I have to get my wife a present.'

'What's the occasion?'

'Anniversary.'

'How many years?'

'She's in her fifties.'

'No, I mean, how many years have you been married?'

'Twenty-five.'

'Congratulations! Right, well, tell me something else.'

'What else?'

'What's your wife like?'

'She's a mother, we have two kids and a dwarf Dobermann.'

'Does she like travelling?'

'No, a trip right now wouldn't be possible… it's a really busy time at work, as I was saying. In fact, I have hardly any time this morning.'

'Would you like to come back tomorrow?'

'No, no, the anniversary is tomorrow.'

'Ah.'

…

'Does she read?'

'Novels. A lot of them, mostly women's stuff.'

'What do you mean?'

'I mean written by females.'

'Hm. Where did you meet?'

'Ostuni.'

'At the beach?'

'Yes, then we got married the next spring.'

'Wow! That was quick.'

'Well, yes... she got pregnant and we got married a few months later.'

'I see. What about something to remind you of when you first met?'

'Yes, fine. Like a swimming costume?'

'No, I was thinking more like something with shells. We could have a piece of jewellery made with shells from the beach where you met. What do you say?'

'Nice. Nice idea but I need to give it to her tomorrow... do you see?'

'Yes, I see. What's your wife's name?'

'Simonetta.'

'Well, given the time restriction... in one day I could go to the beach here and make you a jar with twenty-five shells in it and then maybe we could think of something very romantic to write to her, like a message in a bottle: *Every year, dear Simonetta, I go back to the place that brought us together, pick up a shell and thank the waves that brought me a...*'

'...mermaid! A mermaid is very romantic.'

'...*a mermaid that makes me love every day like the first. Happy Anniversary, star of the sea.*'

'Perfect. OK. Fine. Let's do it.'

'Really? Just like that?'

'Yes, yes, it's fine. She'll love it. You'll make the jar look good, right?'

'I'll make it look nice, don't worry.'

'Like… with something valuable attached?'

'Well… that doesn't strike me as being in the same style as the gift.'

'OK, do this shell-jar thing and the note, which will make my wife weep for joy. But then we need to add something expensive, say around a hundred euros. OK? Otherwise, how will I look?'

'OK, I'm on it. Come back tomorrow.'

'I'll come at 9 a.m., like this morning.'

'I'll expect you at 9.30, then.'

'Goodbye.'

'Goodbye.'

This is what most of my male clients are like. Nothing new.

I send a text to Nicola.

Can you pick up some perfume at the duty-free? A big bottle, fancy name. For a woman.

At least thanks to this guy's request I can go to the beach at sunset with the excuse of collecting shells, and enjoy a bit of nature with no plasterboard behind it.

Mandrill

I lost my head
and found it over the fireplace

I sit back down on the floor, surrounded by all those fake leaves, in a position that is strategic because nobody going past the shop can see me.

Before refurbishing a year ago, in this very spot there used to be the only other thing I kept in the shop, which I've now moved to my living room-studio-bunker.

A sculpture of a giant dick.

It came in a few months after the launch, wrapped in layers and layers of bubble wrap and cardboard. The sender had clearly taken a lot of trouble, and the package had survived a long trip.

There was a note inside:

I went on a course and learnt to sculpt.
Happy?

The ceramic dick was our olive branch, the nastiest, funniest gift I've ever received.

It was confirmation that if Ruth had been the one to open the shop, she would have been brilliant at finding presents for people. Unlike me. She would never have taken the easy route with jars of shells and bottles of duty-free perfume, she wouldn't even have opened the door to a guy like the one who's just left.

But Ruth and I are different.

Some people know how to transform a block of marble, others paint it grey and hide it away in a corner of their life, and others mishandle it until it accidentally breaks. Ruth, my mother and me. Three very different women.

My mother, needless to say, was shocked by the new orna-ment. She was the one who found the perfect place to spirit it away: this blind corner where I'm sitting now, which is practically invisible even though it's in the room.

Considering it's a ceramic phallus in a minimally furnished room, it's always managed to avoid controversy.

Nicola loathes it, too. He says he would never have expected me to like something so vulgar, and that it would be better to keep it at home where no one can see it, rather than on show in the shop.

I tell him that he knows nothing about either chocolate or contemporary art.

When I took Ruth's sculpture home, Nicola had recently stopped leaking tears over his father and forefathers, had man-aged to plug all the holes in his perfect life and was beginning the whitewashing process.

I believe that things are still broken even when they're patched up, because if you look carefully, you can see exactly where the cracks are, no matter how fast or how carefully you picked the pieces up, fitted them together, glued them and left them to dry overnight exactly as the instructions said.

Nicola was a broken record singing 'Marry me, marry me Maria', and there I was carrying home a clay penis. That was when Luigi Fiore came to see me at the shop.

'G'morning.'

'Good morning.'

'May I? Should I have made an appointment?'

'Usually yes, but I'm free right now.'

'Can I sit down?'

'Of course, sit down!'

I feel like we know each other.'

'Yes, Maria, I thought you wouldn't remember. I'm Luigi Fiore.'

'Hm…'

'Gigi Fiore.'

'Sorry, I can't remember where we met.'

'I used to go to swim meets with you, fifteen years ago or so, remember? I'm a friend of Patrizia's.'

'Ah, yes, of course. Gigi. *Ciao!*'

'I saw you'd started this business, congratulations. It's a great idea.'

'Thanks.'

'And Be Present! is a perfect name.'

'I like double meanings.'

'Me too, but not when it comes to people's names.'

'Me neither.'

'Unfortunately my name is Gianluigi.'

We laughed out loud.

'Listen, I'm here because I need to find a present.'

'I imagined that was the case. For who?'

'For me.'

'What do you mean?'

'I came because I'm looking for a present to give myself.'

'This is a first for me…'

'I've just turned thirty and I want to give myself a present. Turning thirty has taken its emotional toll, it's not easy to get used to the idea and I mean… since I don't have high blood pressure or the shakes after the way I've been living the last ten years, I'd say there's a lot to celebrate!'

'I've heard you know how to have a good time.'

'Guilty as charged.'

'It's a talent, knowing how to have fun. Were you looking for something fun?'

'Not just fun, Maria. I want my gift to be unique, price-less, clever, brilliant. And beautiful.'

'That's a lot of qualities for one thing.'

'Yes, I was thinking the same thing. It's amazing how many qualities one thing can have!'

'How much do you want to spend?'

'I fear money can't buy what I want.'

'Gianluigi?'

'Yes?'

'I think I can deliver it quite soon. Does the day after tomorrow at 8 p.m. suit you?'

'Perfect.'

'See you later.'

'See you later. Ah… Maria?'

'Yes?'

'Congrats on the sculpture.'

We went back to smiles, like in a silent movie.

Then he left, jingling the bells above the door.

Deadline

There's no such thing as a horizon

Two days later, at eight on the dot, Gianluigi Fiore crossed the threshold of my shop.

I'd placed a little white box with a red ribbon on the table.

He glanced at it for a second.

He sat down, without saying a word.

He drew the little box closer to him, leaving it on the table. Then he untied the ribbon, slowly, like a person who knows how to savour things.

It occurred to me that Gigi Fiore would never leave a gift in its box, like I did with Mermaid Barbie and every other gift when I was a little girl.

I watched him proceed slowly, pulling one end of the bow then the other, lifting the top slowly, incredibly slowly.

Like people who are hungry but remember their manners and wait politely for the other guests to sit at table and for the conversation to die down rather than throwing themselves at their food, slavering at the mouth.

In the box, there was a key. He took it out and, with the composure of a man who requires neither approval nor confirmation, turned towards the door.

He put the key into the lock: one turn, two turns. He knew exactly what to do.

Then, without turning around, he pushed the button of the roller door, holding his index finger down until the shutter reached the ground with a thump.

That was when he turned and came towards me.

It was 8.05 when he took my hands and kissed them.

My fingers, my nails, my palms, my knuckles, my wrists.

He kissed every part of me. Slowly. Continuing the gift-unwrapping ritual.

He was a real pro. He'd done this before.

Condom ready in the pocket of his jeans, excellent performance, few words.

At 8.43, we were on the armchair, satiated.

It occurred to me that the armchair, which had been responsible for the beginning of the love affair between Nicola and me, had borne witness to its end.

It's turned full circle, I thought. A perfect shape. Just how it should be.

At 8.50 I said, 'I'll be going home in a bit.'

'OK, I'll go, too. Can I say that it was wonderful?'

'If you want.'

'You haven't changed a bit. You're still a bitch and you're still fun.'

'Thanks.'

'You were fantastic in freestyle.'

'I still am, look at my shoulders.'

He kissed them, folding my belly into his arms from behind, resting his head on my collarbone, avoiding the yellow pendant.

Then we got dressed.

'Maria… can we see each other again?'

'No.'

'I thought not.'

'Happy Birthday, Gigi Fiore.'

'Thanks.'

I opened the door he'd locked and lifted the roller door enough to duck underneath.

The logistics were back under my control.

At 9.28 p.m. I was opening my bag and getting my keys out in preparation for reaching my front door as usual. End of fling.

Home, teeth, shower, pyjamas, bread with tomato and oregano, teeth again, computer.

Nicola had the Paris shift that day.

He came in late, when I was already in bed pretending to be asleep.

The following morning, we ate the croissants he'd brought home for me.

Painkiller

Side effects
are written too small

How do people cope with having a lover?

To make love multiplied by two, phone multiplied by two, lie multiplied by two?

My fling with Gianluigi aka Luigi aka Gigi was not a love affair. Far from it.

Those seventy-eight minutes were the direct consequence of a thread running from the place where white light hides all the colours of the rainbow, through London and Ruth, through Adri, through this useless shop where I'm sitting uncomfortably on the floor now, through the moment I buried Nicola's heart and couldn't respond to his marriage proposal.

My betrayal was fidelity, coherence.

It was finally an opportunity to throw away the armchair that Nicola had looked so small and attractive on that evening many years ago, to move the sculpture to my house, to strip the place down to the basics.

And suddenly everything was bare and clean.

That window of time between 8 and 9.18 p.m. was my resolution, the rational and definitive answer I'd been looking for to the question Nicola had been insistently posing. Now I knew what to say.

'Will you marry me?'

'Nicola, last week I had sex with another man.'

'What do you mean?'

'I mean I cheated on you.'

The evening this conversation took place last year, a cupboard door, a glass and a bowl ended up broken.

The door was slammed over and over again, until it wouldn't shut.

The glass fell out of the above-mentioned cupboard into the sink.

The bowl was thrown against the wall, though my face was the real emotional target.

The more crockery that fell on the battlefield, the quieter I grew.

He talked a lot, as usual.

He said things like howcouldyou, yourekillingme, youhave-norespect, he asked things like areyouinlovewithhim? whoisthis-guyanyway? howlonghaveyoubeenseeinghim? comeonconfess.

How I would have liked to light up a cigarette, at that moment, if only I smoked. Instead, I had to sit there at the table, unsure where to put my hands, not looking at anything.

Looking down at the floor would have signified contrition.

At him, defiance.

Filling my eyes with tears, begging forgiveness.

At the ceiling, indifference.

So I chose a random spot to look at. Like ballet dancers when they pirouette, like sailors in a storm so as not to vomit.

I chose the wounded cupboard door and stared at it, listening to the helter-skelter of Nicola's voice first shouting, then breaking, then whispering, rising up again and then swooping down in a nosedive against me.

At a certain point, the fairground ride came to a standstill and he said, 'Talk. You have to talk now.'

Ordering someone to speak is like telling them to relax, all it does is strengthen their resolve to do the opposite.

But I thought that I owed it to him in the end, that I should stop the silent treatment, stop looking at the door, stop reciting how much wood would a woodchuck chuck in my head, that I should turn towards him and say something.

'You're right, Nicola. Tonight, I'll go to my parents' place, and tomorrow we'll talk it over and decide what to do.'

'No, I'm the one who's leaving.'

He said this with an expression I'd never seen on his face. His eyes were filled with the disgust and arrogance of someone delivering a verdict without a trial.

Firealarm

In an emergency, break the heart

Last night at dinner, my mother was talking about Roberta, the woman she and my father were supposed to be going to Marseilles with.

I told her I couldn't remember either the woman or her daughter.

Well, it's only partly true. I hardly remember Alessia, the girl who went to the same school as me, but I do remember her mother. Perfectly.

We were in Caserta on a school trip and Roberta came with our teachers as a parent accompanier. She was one of those keen mothers who was always friendly, amenable, willing, her arms like tentacles, a bit like my mother's. She had nice pert breasts, too.

She helped give out the packed lunches, keep us under control, take the register, stop us from kissing when the coach went into a tunnel.

After going around the Royal Palace, we were supposed to head back to the coach, but I needed to go to the bathroom and so I went to look for one.

My friends always went to the bathroom in twos but not me, because if I know anyone is outside the door, I get stuck and nothing comes out, so I've always preferred to deal with them on my own, my physiological needs that is. To cut a long story short, the day of the school trip, looking for the toilet, I got lost.

I got lost for a few minutes, I think, but evidently it was long enough to raise the alarm with Roberta, who left the group and came looking for me.

I'd turned under the wrong portico and found a little bird.

It was lying on the ground beating its wings, but it couldn't fly. It looked as though it was trembling, or maybe it was actually trembling.

Lying there on the flagstones, inches away from the lawn, in agony and out of place. The bird was lost too.

I bent over its delicate body, it looked as though it was suffering and I thought there wasn't anything for it but to let it die in peace.

But not on the flagstones under a portico when a few inches away there was a beautiful huge garden and blue sky to act as a mirror.

I thought I should move it, but I was scared it might be carrying a disease, maybe something contagious like the illness that killed Ferdinand II, which the guide had been telling us about. I didn't want to risk catching something if I touched it.

So I gave it a little kick.

A tiny, soft little kick. I swear it was more like a gust of wind than a kick, just a way to get the bird to its final resting place.

It worked. It shuffled a little closer. All it needed was another little poke of the foot and it would be on the grass.

That was when Roberta found me, my foot in the air, looking as though I was kicking a dying bird. She gave me the same look Nicola gave me years later, full of contempt, the evening I told him I'd cheated on him.

It wasn't disappointment, no. It was a look that said, 'there, I knew it', a confirmation, a loathing that curled her lips up at the edges, which had always been there, ready to show itself.

Alessia's mother told me with her eyes that she'd always known I was nothing but a little murderess, that everyone knew I'd killed my sister, that torturing animals as a hobby was typical in a future serial killer, that my mother and my father were poor wretches to have given birth to a monster like me, and who knows how much pain I've caused and what a curse it must have been to have had me around all the time and I wasn't worthy of sharing even a packet of crisps with her daughter and how sorry she feels for the poor boy who would be kissing me in the tunnel on the way home.

One look was enough to express all these words in a second, I'm sure because I heard the words so clearly that I turned around on the spot, forgetting the little bird as I was marched off, rucksack on my back, hanging my head, to the coach park where the others were waiting.

It took three long hours to get home, Roberta kept her eye on me from a distance, as I jiggled my right leg nervously, sitting as good as gold in my seat, without kissing anyone in any of the tunnels.

She read these as additional signs of guilt, but I swear my only problem was that I had been needing to pee for hours.

From someone like Alessia's mother, you expect a look like that.

But from someone like Nicola, no. Even if you've cheated on him and even when he's angry enough to break kitchen cupboards and forget his manners.

I thought that look might mean that there was finally a brand-new Nicola standing in front of me, one who no longer needed his heart to be dug up, one who could easily deal with the hole I'd made on the left side of his chest and fill it with something else.

Or perhaps a Nicola who had discovered on his own which tree I had buried it under and was ready to go and get it back and replant it in his body, without needing me to be there.

But no. It was the same old Nicola.

He'd grabbed his case, the one he uses for work, and packed two shirts, two pairs of socks and pants, and his razor. He'd zipped it up noisily, attracting my attention in the hope of being stopped.

But then he did everything by himself.

He stopped by himself. He came back into the kitchen by himself. He found me there, still sitting, and he apologised. Him. He apologised a hundred times. He apologised to me.

'I'm sorry, Maria, forgive me. I've been feeling bad for months, making everything about me. My father... I'm so sorry. I know it's my fault, I know I haven't been close to you, that I'm always working. I know we haven't made love for weeks, that I'm a wreck. And then this thing about getting married... I'm sorry. I've been suffocating you, Maria. I know. But now I get it. I get it and everything will go back to how it was before.'

It must be so hard to live with optimism, it must take so much effort.

I have such respect for anyone who tries, who predicts things will get better, but at the same time such pity. Such pity for you, Nicola.

'I forgive you, Maria. Will you forgive me?'

I should have said he was making a mistake in forgiving me. That I didn't even want to be forgiven. That I hadn't actually asked him for forgiveness. That he had nothing to do with anything. That I hadn't even noticed we weren't making love or that he'd been absent. I should have said that marriage stinks of cut flowers, like funerals. Can't you see it's just an excuse for covering up horrible smells? That you can't go back. That the myth that shrimps walk backwards is not even true. They just jump back when they're scared.

Don't you get it, Nicola? Can't you see that going backwards is always and only out of fear?

But instead, I said, 'Yes.'

He hugged me and lifted me up in his arms.

We went into the bedroom and made love. The following day was Sunday and we spent it in bed.

'Did it only happen once?'

'Yes.'

'Do I know him?'

'No.'

'This afternoon, I'll fix the cupboard in the kitchen.'

'No, don't worry. You can't even see it's broken.'

'I saw you looking at it unhappily yesterday. I'll do it.'

'OK. Thanks.'

'Do you mind if we stay at home today?'

'No, of course not. It's fine.'
'Do you still love me?'
'Yes.'

'Maria, shall we have a baby?'

PART THREE

Lunch

Doublecross

When bricks demolish
rather than build

There's nothing can harm you, with daddy and mammy standing by

That's how the song my mother and father loved so much ends.

One of these mornings
You're going to rise up singing
Then you'll spread your wings
And you'll take the sky

Summer is too beautiful and when something is too beautiful, losing it hurts.

'Take me. I beg you. Take me.'

These were my father's words as he draped himself over the little white coffin, which was so little that it almost disappeared under the mass of a fully grown man's body.

'Take me.'

My father was stuck, too, like my mother the day of the murder, like Nicola one summer evening years later. Each of them tuned into a single refrain.

'Take me.'

I discovered that day that it was possible to shout under your breath because that's what my father did. He shouted without raising his voice.

'Take me. Take me.'

As he repeated this mantra rhythmically, one of the Marias, my mother's mother, led me out of the church.

When we went back in, a good while later, you could only hear the priest's voice and my father had stopped talking. I wonder now whether in all these years he ever started again.

My mother had chosen a monosyllable. Nicola a name. My father, an imperative.

No.

Papà.

Take me.

A response, a name, a request.

Who was supposed to take you, Pà?

And where were you supposed to be taken?

Couldn't you have stayed with us?

I don't know who took you away, but somebody must have done, just like, as you explained a few years later, faxes transport paper.

There was no more dancing in the living room, no more tickling my tummy, no more rides in the trolley at the supermarket. Maybe I did actually grow up, just like that.

My baby teeth fell out and my big teeth grew in. I would wiggle them with my tongue until they hung on a thread, and I wasn't scared because I knew new teeth would soon be coming to fill the gap.

While you, Pà, let yourself be pulled out and taken away by I don't know who, leaving a gaping hole in my smile that would never be filled.

Like the gap left in their mouth when adults fall down the stairs or get their teeth punched out, when regrowing them isn't possible any more.

There are times, though, when losing something prepares you for something new, tougher teeth, more durable, less smooth. That's what you told me, Pà. And then you ate your words.

People say that it's hard for couples to survive the tragedy of losing a child and that it's highly likely they'll separate. My parents, however, stayed together, and were closer than ever.

It's me and my father who left each other twenty-five years ago, like a couple who had stopped loving one another but carried on living under the same roof, to keep the peace and save on lawyers' bills.

So, here's to a happy anniversary to us, too. Let's celebrate with a new ring, silver this time.

At school we learnt that the finger between the middle finger and the little finger was called the ring finger, and that it was the weakest of all.

Let's make it even weaker, then.

Milestone

Used-up videotape ribbon
rewound with a pencil

I pull myself up from the ground at the sound of the bell
jingling.

Shit, I must have fallen asleep for a minute. I cover it up.

'Good morning, Maria!'

'Good morning, Angela. Come in.' I clear my throat.

'Sorry, I'm a bit early.'

'No worries.'

'It's so hot, isn't it? Well, actually, it's hot in the sun... but
cold in the shade.'

'I know. Spring likes to play these tricks on us.'

'You never know what to wear in this weather.'

It's obvious now that Angela never knows what to wear:
she's got on one of those horrendous and expensive down
vests, bright as the LED on the remote when you've just
changed the batteries.

She's a bit tacky too, her eyelids emerald green, hair dyed
a strategic ash blonde to make sure the grey doesn't show
through, and heavy earrings that make her earlobes sag.

If I had to find a gift for her rather than Mr Zaccari, I'd
buy her a pair of sleeves. The thought makes me want to
laugh, but I resist and respond.

'It's true... whatever you put on at this time of year
is bound to be wrong. But spring is a lovely season none-
theless.'

'Well yes, but I'm allergic to olive-tree pollen so it's a nightmare.'

'You wouldn't know it, you look great today.'

'Thanks. It must be because I'm really excited, I must confess. I've never done anything so unusual as coming to a shop like this. I'm really curious to see what you're going to suggest and, most of all, I hope to make a good impression on Mr Zaccari.'

I look her in the painted-green eye and find her touching. I feel guilty I'm not Ruth, that I don't have the dedication needed to fulfil the expectations of all the Angelas in the world, people who are genuinely eager to embrace a different and potentially better version of their lives.

In order to distract her attention from the bluff that I am, I produce the printout I made this morning.

'Here it is, Angela.'

'What do you mean?'

'I mean I've printed a photo of my suggestion.'

'Just one?'

'Yes, because I'm sure it's the right one.'

'Ah, OK. Great. Let's have a look.'

…

'I don't get it. Is it a table?'

'Yes.'

'What are you getting at? I don't understand…'

'It's a walnut table from the late nineteenth century with the finest marquetry. You told me Mr Zaccari's house is beautifully furnished and I think the style might fit well.'

'You know, it really could, even though I've never seen

the house. It reminds me of the wood the letter-holder on his desk is made of. But Maria, I still don't quite understand… How can I present myself at a retirement party with a table? What would the other guests think?'

'You would go to the party empty-handed, in fact.'

'Dear God, how would that make me look?'

'The party is in the office, right?'

'Right.'

'So of course you can't go with the table! We would never ask a man of seventy-four to take home a table as if it were a bottle of wine.'

'No, of course we wouldn't.'

'And anyway, we have to win the auction on eBay and have the table sent over from Toulouse.'

'Spain?'

'France.'

'Dear God.'

'Don't worry, it will get here safe and sound, but we do need to take delivery timings into account.'

'Of course.'

'You'll go to the party unencumbered, because I'm sure all your colleagues have organised a group present with a card brimming with signatures. Am I right? And Zaccari's not going to read them all, is he? Nobody will notice. Then we'll have the table delivered straight to his house, with a nice card signed by you.'

'It's not exactly what I was expecting.'

'I think there's no doubt that Mr Zaccari will invite you round to his house to see where he's put the table.'

'Do you think so? Well, that would be a dream.'

She blushes. '… I mean it would be a dream to see his beautiful house, finally.'

'He's sure to invite you, you'll see.'

'Let me look a little closer… to heck with it! Let's win this auction. It's such a dear little occasional table, with those black and white checks.'

'It's a chessboard.'

'A chessboard included with the table?'

'That's right. But only if you want to play chess. It's just there, without drawing attention to itself.'

'I love chess!'

'I know.'

'How do you know?'

'You told me last time.'

She blushes again. 'But Maria… who knows whether Zaccari plays chess?'

'If he doesn't play, he won't even notice he's resting his elbows on a chessboard. If he does, you could take the opportunity to play together.'

'Maria, thank you. I love it. I thought it was an eyesore, but actually I adore its discreetness, I like its sobriety.'

I look at her flashy vest and realise that objectivity is a rare thing.

'I believe we're on, then.'

'We're on.'

'All I need is Mr Zaccari's home address. I'll keep you up to date on the delivery.'

'Can I send it by email?'

'Of course. I'll send you back my bank details for the payment.'

'Thank you, Maria. I never thought I'd take part in an auction. It's so exciting!'

I smile.

'Can I ask you one last favour?'

'Of course, Angela. What?'

'What do you suggest I write on the card? Do you have a suitable quote?'

'Well… follow your instinct. I'd say we'll miss you in the office and then I'd add something like, "Every day off is… a game won."'

'Very clever…'

I smile again, we shake hands and repeat that we'll be in touch.

How tiring hope is.

Dreamcatcher

Home-made webs
woven by night
to catch the daylight

I should eat more.

This is what my mother tells me and what my Maria grandmothers always told me.

I think women encourage other women to eat more because they hope, deep down, that by making them fatter they'll feel thinner in comparison. As if there's an unspoken competition as to how many bones are on view every time a woman walks through the door.

I rank highly in this type of contest. You can clearly trace vertebra after vertebra down my spine, as well as the squared-off blades beneath my broad shoulders. The lower half of my body is well defined, too, a chiselled network running from my belly to my thighs.

Make no mistake, it's not extreme. Just enough to be called to the podium, not necessarily to win the gold medal.

When I was fourteen, seven years after my sister's death, I went to another psychologist.

She had very black, very curly hair and was the kind of woman who liked flared trousers and stone necklaces. The kind of woman you imagine checking the labels on clothes before buying them, not (like me) because she doesn't want to waste time washing them by hand, but because she has a very low tolerance for synthetic fibres.

She didn't wear glasses and this shocked me. Every session I would check out her eyes, looking for a sign that she was wearing contact lenses.

She must have thought I was hanging on her every word, but actually all I was thinking was that a woman with trousers, necklaces and hair like that couldn't possibly, statistically speaking, have 20/20 vision. You expect a woman who looks like that to wear glasses. Maybe with colourful frames that loudly state, 'I'm short-sighted and I'm not ashamed of it, look at this lovely olive green, or this cool red fence around my eyeballs.' Maybe they'd even be hanging from a chain around her neck so that she could put them on and take them off when required, a gesture that proclaims, 'I'm a woman of substance, practical, interested in being able to see properly in all light conditions.'

Nothing. No sign whatsoever, not on her nose or around her neck. Nor was there a well-hidden, transparent ring around her irises.

I hated her.

She was neither fat nor thin. She was a woman with no adjective to describe her weight.

'Maria, are you eating?'

'Doc, why do you think she made me come here?'

'She who?'

'My mother. She must have told you I don't eat enough, right?'

'She told me she was worried.'

'That's news.'

'How did it go this week?'

'How do you think? I went to school, I ate, I watched *The Simpsons*, I did my homework, I went out on Saturday and it rained on Sunday.'

'How did you feel?'

'Like a pedestrian with no wheels. My mother won't get me a moped.'

'Why do you think that is?'

'Because she's scared I'll die.'

'Because she loves you, maybe?'

'Because she can't fail again.'

'Are you referring to your sister's death?'

'It's pretty obvious, isn't it?'

'Do you think your mother feels responsible?'

'No. It was my fault.'

'Hm.'

'Well? Aren't you going to say it?'

'Say what?'

'Aren't you going to say it wasn't my fault?'

'Maria, there's no need for me to say it. What I need is to understand how *you* feel about it.'

'And I already told you, it was my fault.'

'Yes, I heard you. But do you feel guilty?'

'Doc, I'd prefer to talk about it next week.'

Starting the following day, I stuffed myself, first-course-second-course-fruit every meal, while Homer strangled Bart on the TV.

My mother convinced herself this doctor was brilliant and that I'd been cured.

The following Thursday, the day of my next appointment with the eagle-eyed psychologist, I came down with sudden stomach cramps. Then there was training session after training session at the pool.

The psychologist called home a couple of times. I knew it was her because my mother spoke in a whisper. As if the phone could be wiretapped.

'Apricot, I think you should carry on working with Doctor Pasquale.'

'Ma… I didn't know how to tell you.'

'What, darling?'

'She was always on her mobile during our sessions and I could hardly get a word in.'

'Goodness.'

'I think she wants me to feel guilty about what happened years ago. She led me to believe that what happened was all my fault.'

'Oh no, Maria. You know that's not true, don't you?'

'Yes, Mamma, of course I do. Sorry I only told you now.'

'No, my love. It's not you who should be saying sorry.'

I'm not falling for it, Doc.

That day I even put an extra handful of cheese on my pasta.

The fact is, it's a matter of space.

After my sister died, my mother stuck her inside me.

And where can I find the space for the second helping of risotto, the after-dinner dessert or the snacks between meals?

There isn't room, and it's physically impossible to stuff yourself when you've already swallowed a life and the guilt complexes of an entire family tree.

The universe may well be expanding, but I'm not.

The fact is, it's not a matter of time.

In a documentary on the origins of life, the kind of film Nicola loves, full of long words that could make a toaster manual indecipherable, I heard that time doesn't exist.

The off-screen voice explained that time is relative and that it depends on the relationships between things. And then the voice commented that an astronaut travelling at the speed of light for so many years would come back home younger than his twin brother, who'd been awaiting his return down on Earth. That's exactly what happened to me and Summer, in a certain sense, even though we weren't twins.

I stayed here blowing my wishes onto an accumulation of birthday candles, buying cranberry juice for my veins, paying taxes for rubbish collection and becoming an empty shell who is legally adult.

She, on the other hand, stayed a baby for ever, in her denim dungarees, playing tea parties with her dolls.

Headshrinker

When you come and wash
my thoughts in a bucket
don't shrink them
Dip in for some poems
and recite them to me

In a town like this, there's no point in keeping the shop open at two in the afternoon, especially on a hot or faux-hot day like today when there's no hope of someone coming in. And yet I'm still here.

Nothing happens at 2 p.m.

The lunchtime news theme wafting out of a window, the clatter of plates beginning to pile up in the sink. Other than that, it feels like a test run for civilisation after a nuclear disaster.

So I push the button as if I were hunkering down in a fallout shelter and watch the shutter as it rolls down halfway, just like the heavy eyelids of the men who have gone home for lunch and stripped out of their work clothes as soon as they crossed the threshold.

Just as Nicola's father would have done. He would have peeled off his work shirt and eaten in his singlet on a day like this, bare-chested in summer, in a sweatshirt in winter. In one of those outfits that could be defined as 'home clothes', home being the place where it appears necessary to mortify your body with unflattering garments.

My father was different. When he used to go to the office and come home for lunch, he wouldn't get changed. The only thing he'd take off was his shoes, as we always do in my parents' house. He would stay in his checked shirts and sweaters with leather patches on the elbows.

He would sit at the table in the same clothes as when he sat at his desk writing about an artichoke festival or an exhibition of impressionist paintings.

When he got home, he'd always ring the bell even though he had keys.

He used to play around, coming up with the funniest possible response to the question, 'Who is it?'

It's the big bad wolf! It's Nonna Maria but today I woke up with a bit of a sore throat! It's Gargamel! It's the postman, I need to deliver two little girls!

This last one was what he always said to my mother on the intercom when it was his turn to bring us back home from school. She would be heating up the dishes that one of the Maria grandmothers had cooked for us and delivered in a Tupperware container, both concerned by our mother's limited talent in the cooking department.

I would look out for him outside the gate just after the end-of-school bell rang, and I would always spot him straight away. He was so big, the biggest dad of all.

He'd have Summer in one hand and in the other, the little pink giraffe rucksack she took to nursery school.

She hated school lunches, my sister. When I was at nursery school, they made me stay there all day.

Summer wanted to come home and eat with the rest of us, and that's what she did.

Papà would hook the pink rucksack over one shoulder and hold out his hand for me. He would hold us, one on each side, in a perfect symmetry of arms, legs and ears.

After a few steps, I'd start huffing and puffing, arching my back and pretending to be exhausted.

He got the message right away, slipped my rucksack off my back, and slung it over his other shoulder.

Two shoulders, two bags.

Two hands, two daughters.

Sometimes we would let go of his hand and run little whogetstherefirst races, our school pinnies, mine blue, hers white, unbuttoned and billowing in the wind.

I would always win because, as Papà would say, I was bigger than her.

Thinking how funny our father looked with those two little rucksacks on his shoulders, which were so brightly coloured and out of proportion to his body, makes me laugh.

At one point, they invented school bags with wheels. It was as if they'd invented them especially for me, to replace my father, who only wore pyjamas and never again picked me up from anywhere.

Of course, my mother wanted to buy me one, to lighten my load.

'No way, Mà. I wouldn't be seen dead at school with one of those trolleys.'

'But it's not you with the wheels, apricot, it's the bag. It looks really fresh to me.'

'I think it's crap. And don't say "fresh" if you don't know what it means, OK? If you want to get me something with wheels, buy me a moped.'

'But I've seen lots of kids with that bag!'

'And lots of others with a moped.'

'You'd feel much lighter.'

'No.'

Thinking back, I remember that Gigi Fiore used to have a big sports bag with wheels when he came to swimming practice.

When you were a kid, your sports bag was so embarrassing ☺

I compose the text. I don't send it.

Clockwise

How many hours go by in an empty hour?

Lunch today is a banana. The one I brought from home this morning that's already gone a bit brown.

Fruit doesn't stay beautiful for long after being picked from the tree.

It must be stressful being a piece of fruit, discarded as soon as soon as you show any sign of ageing.

I think fruit must be happier when it's on the tree, hanging onto its branch until it's fully ripe, and then falling naturally to the ground, sowing its seeds. Or carried away in a little bird's belly, flying somewhere unexpected, like a royal palace, in Caserta.

I peel the banana. Looking at it, I'd say I could eat it in four bits, but that's too few. I mentally divide it into ten pieces and nibble my way through it in ten tiny little bites.

Done.

Another meal bites the dust.

Neither my mother nor Nicola understand, they're so apprehensive and obsessive. Opprehensive. I smile to myself.

The thoughts they have that are simple and repetitive are the most dangerous thoughts of all, like those summer hits on the radio. So like one another that you can't remember a thing about them in the end, whether you liked them or not.

It's called the mere-exposure effect, I read it in a textbook at university. It means that the mere fact of seeing or hearing the same thing over and over again makes you begin to like it.

What if they managed to turn me into what they want just by looking at me a lot?

What if they managed to dip their hands into my head and change the wiring of my thoughts?

Tick tock tick tock.

And if, when the bomb was about to explode, I didn't know whether to cut the red wire or the blue one?

Tick tock tick tock.

Over the last week, I've been obsessed with the idea that I might turn into them.

I'm scared. Best to stay vigilant. Though it's hard, given how bored I am. I'm tired of it.

I'm scared of being reassured by certitudes. Scared of becoming like one of those smokers who tell you, through their yellow teeth, never to start smoking, not to make the same mistake they did.

'You're lucky,' they say, coughing up catarrh.

Scared of climbing up to the lectern and still being too short.

Anyway, in this case, too, it would be great if I smoked. Because I could decide to quit and then, as the cliché goes, I could put on weight.

And my mother would stop stressing me out.

I hear a plane flying overhead, in the middle of this tepid silence, and I wonder whether it might be Nicola, on his first return flight from Milan of the day.

In any case, I'm inside and he wouldn't be able to see me in here even if I frantically waved a cotton handkerchief like in those movies about love.

Is this love?

What if it were mere exposure?

Chokeberry

Your sour juice
stains my hands

I met Enrico eight years ago. He was my first client here at the shop.

He came in carrying a leather bag and wearing a midnight-blue woollen sweater. He wasn't wearing a coat, though it was nearly the end of the year.

I thought he was a sales rep of some kind, peddling medicines or airtight jars or hair products, at the door to enquire and propose.

'I'm looking for a gift.'

Amazingly, he'd understood everything, just like that. He was shaking a little.

'OK.'

'It's for my wife.'

Excited, I opened the diary someone had given me at the launch to page one. The paper smelt new and it took me several attempts to separate the leaves.

If I'd been an old teacher, I'd have licked my thumb. Gross.

'Tell me, what's the occasion?'

'Her birthday.'

'Ah, OK. We need to choose carefully. It's always hard to celebrate birthdays over the Christmas holidays, they tend to get overlooked.'

'My wife was born in June.'

'OK. Well, we have time to choose then.'

'No. I need to give it to her today.'

'OK…'

He had big eyes, behind his thick glasses they looked enormous and sea green. Maybe they were watery that day, or maybe they were naturally that way, banks holding the river. He clutched the leather bag on his knees, as if there was a bomb inside.

'My wife told me today was her birthday. She told me the same thing last Friday. I didn't take any notice and she got upset. She threw a spoon at me and said I didn't love her.'

'Sorry, I don't understand.'

'I love her. Of course I love her.'

'Yes, but—'

'I need a gift as soon as possible. I don't know what to do.'

He held onto the bag even tighter.

'OK. No worries. How old will your wife be?'

'You mean today?'

'Um… yes, I think so.'

'I don't know.'

'…'

'She's fifty-seven, my wife Lucia, that is. But today she might be turning forty, or thirty-five… I don't know.'

'We'll be flexible, then.'

A fleeting smile.

I closed the shutter and we walked all the way to Piazza Vittorio Emanuele, where there used to be a well-stocked record shop.

It has now been converted into a tattoo and piercing parlour, which I thought was for the best. Agostino, the owner, had occupied the same space for the last thirty years and I don't think he'd ever had to send anything back to the supplier in his life. The shelves were literally bursting with CDs, cassettes and vinyls.

Enrico, who had told me on the way that he was a doctor, rubbed his chest to keep himself warm. He looked around the shop, careful not to touch anything, as if it were a museum. He seemed disoriented.

'I suggest this one, it's an amazing album.'

'*Colour Green*... never heard of it.'

'It's by a German singer. She recorded it in the early seventies but it only came out in 2006. It came to mind because I'd say it fits, in terms of inconsistency of dates.'

He smiled again, still faintly. 'OK. It sounds like a nice present. My wife loves creative women. She was creative, too. I mean... she is.'

'A singer?'

'No, a painter. She also sculpts. How much do I owe you?'

'Nothing. You're my first customer. It's on me.'

'Thank you.'

'Will you let me know if she likes it?'

'I will.'

'And Doctor, aren't you cold without a coat?'

'Yes, come to think of it. Very.'

He left. With the LP sticking out of his bag, making it impossible to close.

I paid Agostino, got an earful as he read me the riot act for not getting paid for my work, and went back to the shop to doodle in my diary as I recited the seven times table.

Deadpan

I talk to you in my head
I no longer need to speak

I've been suggesting presents for Lucia, Enrico's wife, for eight years. I must have found more than a hundred of them.

It's ritualised anomalous perception, he explained. Every now and again, Lucia is convinced it's her birthday and consequently travels back and forth in time. And she forgets what's going on in the news and how to tie her shoelaces, she forgets how to sign her name or whether Wednesday comes before Friday.

But she never forgets who Enrico is.

I always have a few gifts on standby for her, just in case.

Because her birthday could come unexpectedly and Enrico once told me that he never wanted to feel as bad as he had on that cold morning when we first met. He never wants to miss one of Lucia's birthdays again, whether it's in December or in June, even if she's already celebrated three in the same week.

He never wants to miss her special day. He never wants to disappoint her again.

Lucia's delusions came on unexpectedly and in theory, at this point, they could vanish equally unexpectedly, right? Wrong.

Life never balances out what it gives and what it takes.

This is what my father has never understood. There's no equilibrium, lives are not communicating vessels, there isn't a global waterline to maintain.

Take me. Please, take me.

It was meaningless. Summer could have lived and so could my father. Or they could have both died.

But anyway, I'd like to tell Lucia that the TV news is boring, that shoes with Velcro instead of laces are nice (especially the ones that light up when you walk), that contracts are filled with small print that will always catch you out and that Wednesday, if you think about it, comes both before and after Friday.

And when life is a circle, there's no point trying to put things in order.

There you have it. Lucia proves what I already believed: that there's no such thing as a timeline.

There's space, and she has filled it with gifts to unwrap and hugs to say thank you.

My father has filled it with more space.

I don't think Enrico and Lucia are the fruit of mere exposure.

'Maria, that herb garden was your best yet. Lucia remembered the names of lots of plants just from their smell.'

'I'm really happy. I'd ask you to send my happy returns of the day this time too, but you've never introduced us.'

'Maria, she would forget you.'

'What's wrong with being forgotten?'

'There's a lot wrong with it, I can assure you.'

'But she never forgets you, so you can rest assured.'

'I'm scared. Every time I go home, I'm scared I've been erased, every turn of the key in the lock is a bullet in a game of Russian roulette. I don't know how many more shots are left.'

'Enrico, you need to get out of the house. You must. And anyway, you have your patients… and all the gifts waiting for you at my place.'

'You're right. Speaking of which, Maria, I think the time has come for me to start paying you.'

'If you pay me, I won't work for you any more.'

'If I bring you some old photos, will you create a nice album for Lucia's next birthday?'

'Of course. And Enrico…?'

'What?'

'Why have you two never had children?'

'Because we already have everything, Maria.'

Briefcase

He carried in one hand
everything he needed in a lifetime

My first client was the exception. All the rest are the rule.

What's the point of hanging around here when I already know nothing worthwhile is going to happen?

I switch off the computer, then the lights, close the door and roll the shutter down for the day.

Outside, the desert is as deserted as before.

I throw the banana peel into the bin just outside the shop and ask myself why people are always slipping on them in cartoons.

Summer used to love watching the Pimpa video, and so did I. We loved the way he curled his ears. My sister liked lots of things I liked, I don't know whether she was copying me or whether it was genetic.

She used to like her dungarees which used to be my dungarees.

She used to say everything was hers, but lots of things were mine.

She didn't use to like water, unlike me, who felt at home in it.

We used to have our baths together and she would always cry, she was so scared. She would cry until my parents came and lifted her out of the tub, her chubby legs kicking the air, while I splashed around with my rubber ducks, bubbles and floating books.

She used to like the sand, it made her hysterically happy to roll around in it, sticking all over her body.

Seaside sand, the sand that falls out of the turn-ups of your trousers when it's time to go back to school, the sand that dirties the car, the sand that counts time in an hourglass. Desert sand, which should be covering every boring inch of this town in this precise moment. Personally, no, I don't like sand. Because sand mixed with water makes cement.

I make my way home, get my keys out in preparation, open the door.

I could easily have gone to the airport to have a cup of coffee with Nicola, deceiving him and relieving the boredom of these three long hours that await me.

I can make coffee here, I prefer it made on the stove anyway.

As soon as I put the coffee on, I hear a deep growl.

My belly desperately trying to make itself heard.

Maybe it's the block of marble that has slipped down from my chest.

Though hunger is a more plausible explanation.

Leftover

Come and see
distant civilisations
in pieces
Guess the contents

This is the time of year for deep cleaning.

Spring cleaning, it's called. The time to clean windows, shutters and curtains, sweep cobwebs from ceilings and purge every corner of the house.

Nicola and I don't do these things because I don't want to.

A woman called Rita, or who says she's called Rita, does them. She's from Bangladesh, where I doubt Rita is even a name, certainly not a common one.

She's coming tomorrow, armed with her faithful multi-coloured duster because she claims the cloths that I buy are ineffective against dust.

'Dust doesn't go on holiday, and neither does Rita, Signorina Maria.'

Rita talks about herself in the third person. Which lends credence to my idea that it's a made-up name.

I don't know how to spring clean. I pretend to do the everyday stuff and that's enough.

For Nicola, on the other hand, germs are visible to the naked eye, and in his view, especially around the big holidays, we need a professional to step in.

It's true, Rita is available any day at any hour, just like dust, as she says. She gains huge satisfaction from what she does.

I really don't think Rita, or whatever her real name is, has one of those back stories: that she used to be a heart surgeon and had to reinvent herself in another country to escape war and embrace a lowly cleaning job. Her work is without a doubt her vocation, she hates dust and I sometimes hear her talking out loud to obstinate stains or hairballs.

Mostly she swears she'll wipe them out, issuing death threats against inanimate objects. 'Now Rita's going to eliminate you little creatures. You're trying to hide but Rita has found you!'

I look around the house now and feel relieved in the knowledge that by tomorrow everything will be tidier, everything will be wiped, my fingerprints will be eliminated as if from a crime scene.

Another growl.

I drink the coffee, but it's not enough, nowhere near enough.

Maybe I should eat, I can't faint now, with only two and a half hours to go until the appointment.

I open the cupboard door, the one that got broken a year ago, collateral damage in my betrayal.

Pasta, rice, pasta, beans, pasta, sauce.

I don't like any of it.

I hate the fact that Nicola keeps almost-empty packets of pasta.

If I were the one cooking, I'd mix them all together so that I could finally dispose of those rolled-up bags with less than fifty grams of pasta in each.

But he only cooks one shape at a time, he doesn't contaminate, he doesn't finish.

The leftovers are here in our kitchen, waiting for a twin packet or for the arrival of worms.

Fusilli, conchiglie, penne rigate: I throw out the lot.

Unpopped popcorn left over from the last World Cup: *ciao*.

An old hunk of bread so hard it could break a window: *ciao* to you too.

If he notices, at least it'll be tomorrow and I'll be able to say it was Rita.

A third growl.

I think I really need to get something solid and edible into my system.

I glance around and that's when I spot it.

I pick it up and carry it from the hall, where it was left last night, into the kitchen. I place it triumphantly on the table.

I give it a punch, and then another and another, pummelling it unnecessarily.

I peel the wrapping away and in the shimmering foil I find fragments of chocolate and a plastic bag with the surprise in it.

Punching the Easter egg gives me the same kind of relief we used to feel, Ruth and I, as the train resurfaced at Barons Court. It was so great to be in the light after being underground in the dark. I think that Ruth was actually scared that the sun would be switched off while we were in the tunnel, the same fear that kept us awake at night to make sure that dawn arrived.

We would only get the District Line to go to our favourite place in the city: we called it the Rich People's Line and hardly ever used it. The women on the District Line had the perfect amount of mascara on, a book in their hands, well-brushed hair and subtle jewellery on view.

The contrast was profound between the District Line and ours, where the women looked worn out and carried an array of plastic bags, sometimes even stuffed into an ugly shopping trolley.

This reminds me of Gigi Fiore's wheely bag, and how out of place he'd look on the Rich People's Line.

I tap in the same text: *When you were a kid, your sports bag was so embarrassing*, this time with no smiley, not forcing an interpretation, putting the ball in his court.

Again, I don't send it.

My belly is calling me back to earth, maybe because of the chaos I've created in the kitchen.

I pick up a shard of chocolate, one of the few pieces of a decent size left after my punches, and placate the abyss for a while.

In the plastic bag there's the *luxury surprise*: a fake-silver keychain in the shape of a dog.

Shit! Antongiulio! It's been two days since I last thought of him.

Poor dog. He doesn't know how lucky he is not to exist.

Blueprint

I'm scared of disorder
because sooner or later I find
me

I'm world champion of the quiet game.

The number of words I say to myself in my head is far superior to the ones I allow to vibrate in the air.

Conversely, Summer talked all the time. Sometimes she talked nonsense, other times it was just stupid stuff, little stories she'd made up, or animal noises.

I used to challenge her to the quiet game and she invariably lost.

One afternoon, in that period when my mother had started taking photos of me with her eyes, we were sitting at the kitchen table doing our homework. Or, I should say, I was doing my homework and my sister was messing around with some felt pens in an old diary of my father's. Every time she took the top off one of the pens, she felt a compulsion to tell the whole universe what colour she was about to use, making a silly noise to go with it.

Blue zac zac zac.

Red bruuum bruuum.

Yellow bruuum zac.

'Shall we play the quiet game?'

She happily accepted. She held one hand over her mouth, as if to remind herself she was engaged in a contest, and with the other she carried on drawing abstract shapes that in her mind corresponded to real things, mostly us, the three human beings closest to her.

Finally, I could concentrate on how to divide words into syllables.

RAB-BIT, PAR-ROT. We had to split the word where the two letters were the same.

I looked up from my worksheet and saw her with a finger in the air, the way they'd taught her to do when she wanted to say something.

'No, Summer. You can't speak or you'll lose.'

She went on raising her finger higher and higher, waving her whole arm in my direction.

'No, I said.'

I suddenly realised I'd lost the game. Telling her not to talk was my mistake. And her beginner's luck.

She didn't realise, though. She'd won and she hadn't even noticed. What an idiot.

She went on trying to get my attention, gesticulating wildly, and I persevered in ignoring her. Then a little stream of wee started to run down the leg of her chair, forming a yellow pool on the floor.

Summer went red in the face and started crying desperately.

My father ran into the room and swooped her up into his arms, telling her nothing serious had happened and that she shouldn't worry.

'Maria, might we hear why you didn't take your sister to the bathroom?'

'It wasn't my fault, Papà. She didn't ask me.'

Offhand

Little words, immense avalanches

Ciao, Mary Mine, the early afternoon flight is taking off late. We had to disembark a woman who was off her head. I'll keep you updated. See you this evening.

Nicola's text reminds me of my pewter-grey mother and her fear of flying. I start a new conversation.

So, Mà? Are you going to Marseilles this weekend?

Not even thirty seconds go by before the phone vibrates.

Maybe not, apricot (sad face). Papà has to work (two sad faces). At least we'll have Easter together (smiley face, face with kiss, repeat face with kiss).

I can just see my father lounging around in his dressing gown in the hallway, like a buoy bobbing, signalling deep water.

I can imagine him writing in the paper about all the big events that will be taking place over Easter, the Stations of the Cross and all the candy floss. And my mother making a salad and ordering everything else for lunch from the deli.

And Nicola looking adoringly at me, as he's been doing for the last year or so, as if I were the Virgin Mary.

Then there's me to complete the picture, with my awkward existence, like a Japanese tourist in Piazza del Duomo captured by mistake in a photo portrait of a happy family.

I think it's not going to happen this year, and I don't text back, to either of them.

I go into the bathroom and brush my teeth, then I stick the leftover chocolate in a tin.

I still have a little time before my appointment and so I go into the living room-studio-bunker and write a list for Enrico, so that he can relax for a few more birthdays.

— A snow dome with the Colosseum inside to remind Lucia of your honeymoon in Rome. It will be delivered to your address in four working days.
— A bunch of flowers. Don't ever worry about giving her flowers, even if we've already done so. They're always nice.
— Do you have Scrabble? To remind her of the some of the words that slip her mind.
— A treasure hunt. I'll send you the details by email; I've thought of a nice theme and it's not too difficult.

— *All Men are Mortal*. It's a great book and I think she'll really like it.

— I've almost finished scanning the 1998 slides from your Japan trip. Let me know if you want me to print some out for you.

— *The Platinum Collection 100th Anniversary* by Frank Sinatra. Perfect for dancing in the kitchen.

— They're doing *Orpheus and Eurydice* at the theatre in September. Up for it?

— I've never dared ask before but… a cat? Lucia would be a perfect cat owner.

— Write her a letter. Lots of letters. For other clients, I'd write them but for you I don't need to.

— Her birth chart. I have a friend who could draw it up for her and who could maybe help you in many other ways.

I look at Ruth's sculpture and laugh out loud, like crazy. If I'd been on Nicola's flight today, they would have disembarked me.

I fold the note for Enrico in two and slip it into my bag.

Then I pick up the shop keys, fix them onto the dog-shaped keychain I found in the Easter egg and put them in my bag, too.

Hightail

My life in the saddle
straddles
two centuries
I'm charging out of here

Twenty-five years ago, during the Easter holidays, my parents were doing the spring cleaning, as everyone is supposed to do.

There was a Franco Battiato record playing on the hi-fi, the one with the song about a solitary beach, the centre of gravity, a white flag, birds like planes.

It's a short LP, I think. Because I remember the same songs playing over and over again, on a loop.

The Maria grandmothers had been busy all week revelling in prayers, chants, holy sepulchres and cakes in the shape of doves, enjoying what had always been for them the highlight of the year.

'Fly Away Dove' was one of the first songs I ever heard, and I don't think I've ever heard it anywhere but at my grandmother Maria's house, my mother's mother, that is. I've never heard a professional recording of it, on an album, I only know it in my grandmother's voice. She missed out lots of words in the verses, and she would sing the chorus any number of times. It was an integral part of her Easter playlist, no different to the interminable Hallelujahs, Great Vigils and Services of Light.

Pray, my soul is mad, my grandmother would belt out as she beat eggs and sugar together.

'SAD, not mad!' my uncle Giorgio from Milan, who's always been a pedant, would correct her.

Thank God my uncle and aunt from Milan, Francesca aka Kekka and her husband Giorgio, only *came down south*, as they would say, for Easter, while they spent Christmas in the mountains, breaking my grandmother's heart. I haven't seen them in the flesh for years, but they call often.

After Summer was born, we would go less often to the grandmother Marias' houses. Instead, they came to us.

At the time, my mother worked as a nurse. But she's been the manager of a shoe shop now for more than twenty years.

That Easter week we were not there for the grandmothers' furious preparations, having made plans to gather together as a family on Easter Sunday for the annual lamb slaughter.

My parents were out on the balcony.

My mother was washing the shutters while my father was having a look at the rolling mechanism that had been broken for ever, depriving our living room of proper daylight.

Summer and I were playing in our room.

Flyover

I'm scared of swallows
because sooner or later they fly
away

175

My earliest memory is of my mother vomiting.

We were on our own at home and I was scared.

She stroked my hair and said with a smile that she was fine and that soon a little brother or sister would be coming along.

I remember that smile on her pale face perfectly, torn between joy and pain. Undecided, as always.

She was on her knees in the bathroom, with her uniform still on, those white clogs with little white holes in them that people wear in hospitals.

I was confused because it seemed as though how she was feeling and what she was saying didn't match up. But most of all, I didn't see how it was possible that a baby could be at once a little brother or a little sister.

'Are you happy, apricot?'

'Mamma, I'm a little girl, aren't I?'

'Of course you are, darling.'

'Are you sure?'

'I'm sure. Come and sit on the floor here with me.'

Doublebreasted

Cufflinks on wrists refusing to shake hands

I'm tired. I've been really tired for days now.

I'm already out, with enough time for a detour.

Mine and Ruth's favourite place in London, joint with the Buddhist temple that fed us, was Kew Gardens, a huge park with every imaginable variety of plant, tree and flower.

It was the only place we were willing to pay an entrance ticket for, the only place that was worth taking the Rich People's Line for.

Adri used to tell us we were stupid to go all the way out there just to lie on the grass, since there were hundreds of parks much closer to our hostel. Adri used to say we were stupid to pay money to look at flowers.

But the reality is that we never stopped for a second when we were in Kew Gardens. We would walk and talk, or walk and not talk, letting go of imaginary balloons, taking the weight off our chests as they flew up into the sky. Peripatetic philosophers with no school of thought to our name, we would run through our brief but insatiable lives as we walked among the trees. There was no need to impose the quiet game on Ruth. It was as if, at a certain point in our wanderings, the impulse to start the game was telepathically transmitted between us. We would often start talking again at the same time, tripping over one another's words, and it made us giggle so much that we almost forgot what we had wanted to say. And yet, moments before, the words had seemed so urgent, so important to communicate.

On leaving the park, we would read a few palms to earn back the entrance ticket and Tube ride.

Going home was harder, because the train started out overground but then, inevitably, dove down below.

I find myself in front of the post office without knowing how I got here. Sometimes I think our legs walk on their own when they are in sync with our thoughts.

The stabs of pain in my belly are not getting any better, thank God it's only two hours until my doctor's appointment.

I take the ticket with the picture of a package on it from the machine.

There's not much of a queue, there never is in the afternoon, and I wonder why my Maria grandmothers insisted on coming here in the mornings, wasting a lot of time that they could have saved.

Thinking about it, maybe that's what they wanted. To kill time.

Waiting for my turn, I buy a yellow bubble-wrap envelope.

I tear a page out of the diary I keep in my bag:

Ruth Ruta

These are for you. You know the address already. Do what you want with them.

The clients are all pretty awful, with the exception of one man, who will of course be your absolute favourite of all time and all places.

Test of our old friendship: if I had an imaginary dog and I entrusted it to you, would you feed it? He's called Antongiulio and there's an image of him on the keychain.

P.S. The sculpture was really great.

Hangover

By taking away
and taking away again
our life is on the hook

The day our parents were on the balcony dealing with the living-room roller shutter, my sister and I were in our bedroom.

Some friends at school told me they had a room of their own, and their little brother or sister had a different room. That was not the case for us. It seemed to me that, statistically speaking, it was a matter of gender. If siblings were brother and sister, it was more likely they would get a room each. It wasn't a matter of available square feet.

Summer was wearing her denim dungarees that used to be mine but didn't fit me any more now that, I don't know how, I'd grown bigger.

My sister liked talking so much that she couldn't understand why inanimate objects like animals and plants didn't have a voice. So she dubbed all their conversations.

If we passed a dog on the street, she would desperately need to specify what state of mind it was in.

Maria, that dog is really happy. He told me so!

I would sometimes hear her talking to the basil plant in the kitchen.

Aren't you bored sitting here inside all the time, little plant?

And then, in a different voice, *Hey, little girl, I walk around at night when you're all asleep. Lazybones. Lazybones!*

She used to laugh, as if she were amazed by her own words.

Complete verbal communication, with vocabulary and syntax, was a new tool, and as her most recent acquisition, she wouldn't let it go for a moment.

She gave names to objects.

Her favourite cup was called Pippi, her pink giraffe rucksack was called Armando, and she had a flowery raincoat she called Olga.

We were supposed to remember them all.

'Mamma, Maria took Pippi.'

'Maria, give Pippi back to Summer.'

'What are you talking about. I haven't got her blanket.'

'That's Luisa. Pippi's her cup.'

My father used to say that my sister would be a sports reporter, providing minute-by-minute commentary. He said there weren't many women in the field and he couldn't understand why.

That afternoon, I was focusing on my building set. I'd received it for Christmas from my uncle and aunt in Milan.

But I'd never opened it. I wanted to put it together before I saw them at Easter lunch, because I was sure they'd ask me if I'd liked it and I didn't want to be unprepared.

The picture on the box told me I was supposed to build an ice-cream parlour with a yellow cash register and a lilac counter. In the box there were two female figures: a blonde lady in a pink uniform and a little girl in a white T-shirt and shorts. The ice-cream vendor and her customer. They looked similar, I thought they could be mother and daughter. But ultimately all the plastic figures looked alike and it didn't mean they were related.

And anyway, I thought, if the ice-cream vendor were her mother, she wouldn't be selling a cone to her daughter. The little girl would have been able to eat as much ice cream as she wanted if that had been the case. Without paying. Lucky her.

Summer had put all her favourite soft toys in a circle and she was having a pretend tea party with them.

Every animal had a miniature teacup set in front of them, while my sister, for herself, had chosen Pippi, her official cup.

She was doing different voices for all the guests, conversing with them about nursery school, Nonna Maria's new oven, monsters they might meet in the night and that would disappear when they wake up. They were talking up a storm.

I mean, I know it was only her talking but it was as if a whole orchestra was accompanying her. As if Summer had always had a whole film inside her, with its own soundtrack.

She took sips of her pretend tea, making that horrible tight-lipped sound. The same sound as when you suck in a strand of spaghetti before you learn to do it properly.

I had to concentrate on my building to shut out all that noise.

There weren't that many blocks to put together. I had to tell Aunt Kekka that she could get a more advanced set next time.

Bruno Bear, what's your favourite colour?

Yellow? You too? Just like me! That's so great!

I started thinking of long words in my head and dividing them into syllables, trying to think louder than all of Summer's teatime chit-chat.

How do you divide 'incomprehensibility' into syllables?

I think it's seven.

Pippi, I'm starving. What shall we eat with the tea?

No, it's eight syllables.

When we went back to school, I'd tell my friends I'd found a word with eight syllables. They'd be so jealous.

Forget rab-bit and par-rot.

Silence, at last.

I finished putting the ice-cream parlour together.

Then I turned and saw her on the carpet.

Her soft toys must have suggested she had a rest.

Boring. Maybe I should go out and wash the windows, listen to the radio on the balcony with Mamma and Papà.

The set my aunt and uncle had given me was really far too easy. I took it apart and started putting it away.

I noticed immediately that there was a piece missing.

The one shaped like an ice-cream cone, with a round base that could be slotted onto the counter.

It was gone.

I moved closer to Summer and touched her feet to tickle her. She didn't laugh. She didn't move.

I looked at her face. A colour I'd never seen before. On a face, that is.

It was the colour of the sky, of the sea, of denim, of the most terrible mistakes.

If I count to three and she still isn't talking, I'll go and call Mamma and Papà.

One, two...

PART FOUR

Teatime

Checkmate

From the top of the tower
I see
the pattern

My grandfather had a boat called *Liberty*.

And, for this, my grandmother never forgave him.

He used to go out fishing, my father's father, and he loved the sea more than anything else.

His job, though, was to sell household linen door to door. Sheets, pillowcases, tablecloths, tea towels. He would knock at the door of women who couldn't wait to embroider a daughter or niece's initials onto them, so that they could give them a pure white, well-ironed future. These women would set aside enough towels to dry the Amazon River in one go, buy so many nightdresses that one lifetime would not be enough to wear them all.

A son, on the other hand, was expected to bring kitchen-ware to the marriage, especially saucepans. Which they would never use, because their wives would be the ones in the kitchen, the women's realm.

My grandfather wasn't interested in providing for sons. In the calculation that was (and is) marriage, crockery plus linen, he was concerned only with the second addend.

Apparently he was brilliant. Always doing good business.

I've never met him but everybody says I'm just like him.

I think that's why my grandmother lent me the money to open the shop, because she was convinced it would be a success, just because of these fleshy, slightly pursed lips of mine that look just like his.

That boat was the source of a great deal of unhappiness for my grandmother. Starting with its name, which wasn't hers. It wasn't even the name of a saint that might protect him at sea.

It was a stupid made-up name that had nothing to do with her, nothing at all, and in choosing it, her opinion had not even been consulted.

'Where on earth did he fish that name from?' was one of my grandmother's set phrases. I must have heard her repeat it at least a thousand times, whenever she talked about her husband, which was very often.

I've always been her redemption in that respect, I know it. She got her own back for not having had the honour of the five modest letters of her name painted in blue on the white wooden boat that would take the greatest love of her life out to sea.

My grandfather was always tanned. Always smiling. Always light-hearted. And in this respect, no, we are not alike. But I swear my lips look as though they've been sliced off his face and stuck onto mine, and this was enough for me to win a childhood of concessions, precious promises strung into garlands and placed around my neck. Pearls of expectation to fulfil.

We were like two blocks of prized marble, never sculpted.

The lips of my grandfather, the name of my grandmother and guilt stuck on my forehead, a brightly coloured Post-it with one word on it. That was my lot in life.

A sumptuous trousseau had been prepared for my sister and me, too, before we were even born.

It's divided into two trunks, in my parents' garage.

The choices were down to one.

I'd never make a dowry chest for my daughter.

If I had a daughter, I'd call her Liberty.

Butterfly

Laws
neither of religion nor of humankind
Laws
that move the universe

I've known I'm pregnant for more than a week.

I did the test with the two little bars, like you see in films.

I couldn't say no to Nicola, after cheating on him. But I couldn't say yes, either. So, I didn't say anything, not even then.

Things went their own way and nothing happened, exactly as I'd imagined. I've always thought I wasn't fertile. I've always been convinced that no independent human being complete with all its component parts could possibly come out of me.

Months went by and nature was proving me right.

Then nature went crazy, there was a bug.

I remember New Year's Eve in 2000. We were at home in our pyjamas. My father was looking at the fax machine and the computer as if they were about to blow up. When midnight struck, nothing happened. So we opened a bottle of Prosecco in that dust-covered spirit of melancholy that ushers in every new year.

Perhaps a little disappointed that disaster hadn't struck.

I thought this was the same, that the greater the scare-mongering, the less likely you are to derail. The greater the prize, the less likely you are to win. The prophecies of charlatans, I thought.

Like the palms I used to read in London, pulling predictions out of thin air.

If I were an indie singer, that would be my name, Thin Air.

In short, I peed on the stick and, well, the instructions are so basic that the situation was pretty clear pretty quickly.

Then I thought about smokers, again. About how difficult it must be for a pregnant smoker to stop. Just like that, from one day to the next. Then I thought of backstroke, how it must be the most comfortable style if you're pregnant. Ruth, once again, had been one step ahead.

She was right about everything.

You don't need eyes to swim. In fact, eyes trick, cheat, give away.

Ruth has an inner compass, hidden somewhere like one of those microchips you see in sci-fi films, implanted under the skin. A compass that always takes her in the right direction.

Let it be backstroke then. But what if I prefer freestyle because of the name?

Nicola was flying that day.

I threw the plastic stick that looked like a thermometer into a bin on the street and went to get a haircut.

I hate having to get my hair cut, having to take care of it.

I thought I'd take advantage of my confused state to tick this annoying task off my to-do list. And in the end it wasn't so bad. It's a bit like pregnant smokers having to give up. At least they don't have to worry about getting fat when they stop because the weight gain is going to happen anyway.

Thinking about it, getting pregnant is a great strategy for limiting the collateral damage of giving up smoking.

'Mary Mine, this new haircut really suits you.'

Aboutface

I'm extreming
You're extreming

My number flashed on the display. I hand the yellow package to the man behind the counter.

'All the way to Florida, eh?'

Why are postal workers always amazed when you give them something to post? Isn't that the main reason for their existence? To send things far away?

Although when I think about it there are people who are shocked when you use your phone to make calls rather than text or look up a famous actor's date of birth.

We often forget the origin of the things we hold in our hands, the original requirement that started everything. We're so anxious to keep up with ever-more sophisticated systems, to cloud our vision with all the extras.

My grandfather's boat had two oars and nothing else.

The fact is that when you use your phone to send a text or a voice message, you're strategically avoiding risk. The risk of having to answer back, improvise, react to the other person. Of having to think on your feet.

A one-way flow of information.

My grandfather's boat had an unpredictable interlocutor: the sea.

'Yes. It's going to Florida. When will it get there?'

'Hm… who knows? I'd need to check. Do you need to know?'

'No, it doesn't matter. Send it anyway.'

He puts it in the box.

I crumple the ticket with my number on it in a ball and throw it into a cylindrical thing by the door.

Which should be a wastepaper bin.

But could be an umbrella stand.

Water or paper?

There are other tickets in there so it must be the right place.

Let it be a wastepaper basket then, because there are precedents and I'm following suit.

It still looks like an umbrella stand to me.

Can you tell me what you are, black plastic cylinder?

What purpose were you born for, and have you just betrayed it?

Scarecrow

Don't let me fly back

From the post office to the hospital takes about forty minutes on foot.

My mother often wears heels, she says they're more comfortable than flat shoes and she can walk as fast as a parcel on its way to Florida in them.

I don't. I nearly always wear boots because I don't like trainers but I'm better off nearer the ground. Maybe that's why I've always chosen swimming, one of the only sports where trainers, so excessively technological, so garish, so tight-fitting, so laced-up, aren't needed.

Feet should always be free.

Nicola wears shoes even when he's at home, what a pain that must be. I take them off as soon as I can, even on a train, at a restaurant, in the shop.

They say when you need to feel someone else's pain you should put yourself in their shoes.

You can see how different people are from their shoes much more than from their clothes. Shoes tell you everything about the people walking around in them. When I used to pretend to read people's palms, I'd try and guess what they wanted to hear after looking closely at their feet, creating a personality profile for them starting from their lower extremities.

In London, nobody cared whether I had my shoes on or not. Maybe that's why I felt at home there.

What would you call someone who doesn't want to wear shoes? A barefooter? A perfect word for places with lots of green lawns to run on, not for here.

If I have to choose a way to trap my feet, boots are perfect because you can take them off in a second, they wear out but they last, they make a noise but they're not too loud and they protect your feet from the rain.

It's not raining today.

I'm exhausted. Against exhaustion, there's no sole that's up to the task.

This forty-minute walk feels impossible.

I don't want to take the car because the doctor said I shouldn't drive today. So I make a revolutionary decision: I'll take the bus.

It's 4 p.m.

I wait on the bench outside the post office.

At 4.20 I see it coming. Half-empty, slow, painted an orange that doesn't exist anywhere other than on the exterior of buses in towns like this. Pantone should call it Bus Orange. A few old people get off, with bills to pay and letters to send, clinging exaggeratedly to their bags.

Nobody gets on besides me.

I stamp the ticket that I bought at the newsagent, which causes a stir.

There are only old people on this route. I doubt anyone actually pays for the ride. Everyone exempted by age, except me.

One woman has one of those shopping trolleys. I look at her and smile. She gave in and bought one, but I forgive her.

Another woman is fanning herself with a pile of red and white papers that look like doctors' prescriptions.

Right at the front, there's a man in a smart hat, sleeveless sweater and tie. A little stooped, very polite. Men of a certain age always dress as if they're going to a party, even when there's nothing to celebrate.

We set off, like a rather strange school trip.

I look out of the window and think of all the songs we used to sing on the bus, singing them so loudly in my head that I'm scared other people can hear.

Ten green bottles hanging on the wall… and if one green bottle should accidentally fall, there'd be nine green bottles hanging on a wall.

I remember our trip to the Royal Palace in Caserta, Roberta, the wounded bird.

I think, for the first time in all these years, that I made a mistake.

I should have helped it properly. I was wrong to back down under Alessia's mother's gaze and not nudge it all the way to the lawn. I made a mistake.

A small chip has just come off the marble block on my chest. I'll leave it here on this plastic seat, for the next person who needs an anchor to stop them from floating away.

Moonshine

Half empty or half full
it doesn't make any difference
You're always a hundred per cent thirsty

We've reached our destination.

The hospital is the end of the line, so we all get off, nearly all. The man in the smart hat stays on board.

Maybe this circular route is his merry-go-round and he wants another ride.

I think about what my life would be like if I stayed on board, too. If I went back to where I started.

But a destination is a destination. The journey is just the length of time it takes to figure out where you want to go. But figuring it out isn't enough. You need to actually get there.

Nicola and the man in the smart hat would be great friends, so preoccupied with transporting their bodies through space that they are satisfied by the motion itself.

I wonder what my grandfather went out in his boat to do? My father said he never caught a thing. I can see him sitting there at sea, smiling with those full lips that are so similar to mine, thinking about how things could be different. As he imagines the weddings of the young daughters and nieces of his clients, fantasising about some of them, a friendly fish swims by. I can see my grandfather observing it, letting it swim away freely.

I go in. The doors open automatically in front of my body.

It feels strange, today, being detected by the sensors, being perceptible, visible, real. Existing.

The doctor told me to come in through Accident and Emergency if I wanted to keep a low profile.

He told me to wait for him at 5 p.m. on the dot in front of the lifts and that he would come and get me.

It looks like a quiet afternoon, in terms of trauma.

There are a few people moaning, a boy on a stretcher who looks perfectly conscious and a mother rocking a little boy who's crying.

No blood and guts here.

A nurse with giant breasts asks me if I need anything.

I say I don't, that I'm waiting for a doctor. Then I look away.

Damn. I should have waited outside. What am I going to do here impaled under everyone's gaze for three minutes?

Damn those doors that recognised me and let me in.

If I smoked, I'd go outside and light a cigarette. Going back in time and picking up the habit feels like a good idea right now.

I lean on the wall and start singing in my head, but I can't think of a single decent song except 'Fly Away Dove', and I can't remember the words.

The little boy starts crying louder. His mother gets up and walks with him, right past me.

I wonder whether we feel pain more keenly as kids or whether we simply learn to contain it better as adults.

The mother smiles at me with that smile mothers with kids always have. A smile that demands empathy from all the actors in the scene, and from all the elements of the universe. Putting on a show. But you don't need to make an effort. You're a beautiful pair even when one of you is crying and the other's hair is a mess. And you know it. Damn you, too.

I don't smile back. I pretend to look for something in my trouser pockets, as if my phone is vibrating.

I take it out and open and close my contacts, open and close my email, open and close the calculator.

3 minutes x 32 years − 25 + 50% probability divided by 5.

My screen says its 5 p.m. exactly.

If he's late, I'm leaving. I can't stand it any longer.

But he's not. There he is. Of course.

There he is in front of the lifts in crumpled blue scrubs and the same white clogs with little holes that my mother used to wear when she worked here.

Punctual. Super punctual, as always.

'Ciao, Maria.'

    'Ciao, Enrico.'

Handsome

In a hurry to give a caress

'Your scrubs are creased.'

    'Don't change the subject, Maria.'

    'Change? This is the first thing we've said to one another.'

    'Yes… but you know what I mean.'

    'Actually, I don't.'

    'Do you think it's the time to talk about my scrubs?'

'OK, let's not talk about them. I didn't think it would upset you so much.' I start laughing. He doesn't. '…in my next list of presents for Lucia shall I add an iron?'

I try again. He's not going for it, not yet anyway.

    'Maria.'

    'Enrico.'

    'You know that what we're about to do is wrong.'

    'I didn't think you were so moralistic.'

'I mean it's wrong bureaucratically speaking… you should have come in this morning and we should have admitted you. Did you bring your tests?'

'Yes.'

'Good. Let's at least try to do everything else properly.'

He's nervous. He reminds me of the day I met him for the first time. The words he's saying make sense if you put them in the right order. They do. But it's as if they've been jumbled up and put in single file, different lives meeting by chance in the queue for the cashpoint.

A mechanical female voice says *Lift going up* as the doors close.

I feel like answering with a phrase like *Guitar playing* or *Cow Mooing*, but I realise Enrico isn't in the mood for surrealism today.

'Do you have any symptoms in particular?'

'I don't think so… I'm not exactly an expert. I'm really tired.'

'Tiredness is a normal symptom.'

'OK. I think I'm hungry as well.'

'That's normal, too. Any spotting?'

'What?'

'Blood.'

'Oh no, no blood.'

Doors opening, the disembodied voice says.

It's not lying, the doors do open. Onto a corridor that is identical to the one we were in before. As if, basically, we had never moved.

'Follow me, Maria.'

'OK.'

I follow him as far as a closed door. He has the keys.

We go in. It's an ugly little room.

There's a bed, an armchair with wheels on it and a cupboard. That's all. It feels even less furnished than my shop.

Though my walls painted with jungle scenes are much better than these dirty yellow ones.

It's a grimy colour, a waste of yellow, sad in the way that only beautiful things that have been abandoned can be. A disused fairground.

Hospital Yellow on the Pantone palette. A page that should be torn out of the paint catalogue.

Enrico closes the door behind him.

He gestures for me to sit on the bed. I obey and, even though I don't think it's required, take off my boots.

In American films, there's often somebody lying on a bed wearing shoes. How awful is that?

Whenever my father watched films like that my mother and I would protest against the screen. Sometimes with the dangerous collateral damage of talking over a few exchanges in the dialogue. If that happened, my father would push the button with the double back arrow and rewind. He's always hated missing any part of the plot.

He's always had a button he could push to rectify the situation. In films, that is.

'You didn't need to take your shoes off.'

'I know, Enrico. I thought not.'

Dogfish

> I threw the shark a bone
> I bought him a lead
> I took him to the park
> But it's no use
> It's not working

'Let's look at the tests, shall we. Do you have them?'

'Yes, I have them.' I hand him my phone.

'On your mobile?'

'Yes, the lab sent them by mail. You're very nineteenth-century today.'

And there it is, the faintest hint of a curl of the lip. Could it be a little smile for me?

He mutters as he swipes at the screen with his finger.

'Everything OK?'

He mutters some more.

'Enrico, is everything OK?'

'Yes, yes, everything looks normal.'

'That's good.'

The phone rings. Mine, while it's still in his hands. Enrico looks alarmed and his face confirms that it's Nicola calling. I grab the phone from him and reject the call.

'Maria, you haven't told him, have you?'

'If I'd told him, do you think I would be here in secret?'

I was sure Nicola would call me at this time, that he

wouldn't be able to resist after spying the appointment in my calendar.

I tap: *In shop with client. Safe flight. See you tonight.*

I send the text.

He can't correct me without humiliating himself, which means he won't.

'Maria, he has the right to know.'

'Did you know that people who work in hospitals are the most likely to cheat on their partners?'

He looks at me, appalled.

'I mean, there are a lot of extramarital affairs in hospitals. I mean, among colleagues.'

I'm saying 'I mean' too much. I'm nervous. I think.

He continues to observe me, looking perplexed, as my feet dangle off the edge of the bed.

'It's absurd, isn't it? Just think, another high-risk category are pilots. I mean, for example, affairs between flight assistants and pilots go on all the time. And yet you and Nicola are probably two of the most faithful men I've ever met. Absurd.'

He seems to have lost his voice.

'I mean… Enrico, I was intending to pay you a compliment. Or at least I think I was. The thing is, I had a haircut and while I was waiting I had to read a few magazines.'

…

'Maria, how about we focus on you for a minute? OK?'

'OK.'

He starts talking to me like I've never heard him talk in the last eight years. Clearly, very clearly, slowly.

As if he's onstage reading a warning label and you unex-pectedly find yourself paying attention.

He uses all the right words, the technical words burnished by his profession, but he pronounces them so clearly, mimes them with the obvious desire to communicate effectively, that I'm sure anyone would be able to understand him.

'Is that all clear?'

'Yes.'

'Right. Repeat it.'

'Really?'

'Yes, repeat everything I said.'

'Is this how you treat all your patients?'

'I choose the most effective method for the person I happen to be dealing with.'

'And who are you dealing with today? A student?'

'No. A woman who understands things better when they come out of her own mouth.'

'Do I really have to regurgitate everything as if I were at school?'

'Yes.'

It makes sense. After all, the other place where betrayals are very frequent is at school. So the magazine said.

Copycat

Purring then hissing
Afraid of feeling

'In a nutshell, I take these pills. You weren't supposed to give them to me without admitting me but you're giving them to me anyway because you're fond of me and you feel you owe me something.'

'I never said that.'

'You should have.'

'Go on.'

'I have to take the three pills together and, two days later, I should come back here to the hospital and you'll give me something else to take.'

'Is that it?'

'No. After a couple of weeks, I'm supposed to come and see you to make sure everything went as it should. To begin with, I may feel a bit unwell, have cramps, nausea, diarrhoea, and other stuff. In two days' time, though, things will get much worse and I'll have actual contractions and there will be a lot of blood. If I have any other problems, I should call you. The end.'

'I'd never have put it that way.'

'Indeed, you said it much better.'

'OK. It sounds like you've understood.'

'It wasn't hard.'

'How are you?'

'Is it relevant?'

'Absolutely.'

'I don't know. But I think I'll find out.'

'Take all the time you need. Any other questions?'

'Yes.'

'What?'

'Did Lucia like the balloon?'

'On the subject of the procedure?'

'In order to feel calm before going through with the procedure, I'd like to know whether your wife liked the balloon.'

'Yes. She loved it. She laughed a lot when she saw it, she remembered an episode when she was a child that she'd never told me about before.'

'Good. I'm happy.'

'Maria, are you sure?'

'About doing it?'

'Yes.'

'I think so.'

'We can drop the whole thing.'

'No.'

Beeline

I get lost all the time
But I always know which way
the sea lies

Enrico and Lucia never had kids because they already had everything. That's what he told me.

For a week, I've been asking myself what Nicola and I have.

Apart from our imaginary dog, our house that we don't like, our jobs that strain our backs and our minds, the words that we should have said many times but that have piled up under the carpet, making the floor a trip hazard.

Maybe Enrico is wrong. Maybe the truth is that it's precisely once you have everything that you can allow yourself to have kids.

Maybe I don't want to have a baby because I still don't have anything.

In the pocket of the crumpled blue scrubs there's a little box.

Enrico hands me the box.

I open the box.

Inside there are some pills.

There are three pills.

The pills are a grimy yellow like the walls of this hospital.

Enrico says I have all the time I need to think about it.

He says I'm not obliged to do it.

He says there's nothing wrong with taking my time or changing my mind.

He says that I need some privacy.

He says he's going to do a round of the ward so that he can give me some space.

He says he'll be back in a bit and we can talk some more.

He says I don't need to decide today.

He says all these things without looking me in the eye.

I deduce that the words are for me anyway.

Enrico goes out, closing the door behind him.

I'm alone in this horrible room, where I don't know where to lay my eyes.

The room feels smaller than before.

I have all the time I need to think.

As I've been told.

I rest my eyes on the yellow wall.

No, I'm not doing that.

I rest my eyes on my socks.

That works.

I start thinking.

Seesaw

My words swing
up and down
making me seasick

Question 1

What happens if I take the pills and tell everyone I had an abortion?

Essay

'Mà, I've got something to confess.'

'What is it, apricot?'

'I got pregnant and I had an abortion.'

With these words, the heavens open and a pot of dark paint is tipped over her head. The paint pours down her head, then her face, then slowly down her clothes and finally reaches the high heels she's so good at walking in. My mother's greys turn irremediably to slate. Then with her hands she scrapes the paint from her eyelids to free her leaden eyes so that she can snap the last of her imaginary photos.

Snap.

The last photo in her album of memories is of my dumb face waiting in vain for her to say something.

Mother, I'd like you to understand but the point is that I wouldn't know how to explain it to you.

Mother, I'd like you to know that I've never killed anything in my life. Ever. Not then, not now.

We'll lighten your greys, once again, Mother.

And we'll look for more white paint, I promise.

There must be more somewhere!

Mà, say something.

Mà, wait. Don't go. Don't be a wave.

If you wash away, you have to come back, OK Mà?

I know this doesn't make sense to you.

But I'm different, Mà. A different person to you. I'm not you.

Don't you think there should be a moment when I can start living too?

Mà, I swear I'll do my best.

No, Mà, doing one's best and making a sacrifice are not the same thing.

Mà, don't get them mixed up.

Mà, I beg you, don't buy flowers for me, too.

It's no use. She's gone.

'Roberta, there's something I need to tell you.'

'What is it, you little criminal?'

'I got pregnant and I had an abortion.'

'Of course you did. There you go again. Your sister, the little bird, your baby. Nothing could be more obvious. I'll go and pick your parents up and take them to Marseilles. While we're away, please pack your bags and leave. Get on a coach and go somewhere else, and don't kiss anyone in the tunnels, don't ever touch anyone again. Because you see, my dear, you can't control yourself and you end up pregnant, and you'll do it again. And during the Easter holidays of all times, you little premeditating bitch. Your poor mother.'

Roberta, I'd love to learn to play buraco just so I can see your face when you win. Just so I can read in your eyes how satisfied you feel when you count up the points and write them down in your notebook.

Congratulations.

Clap clap.

'Lucia, I had an abortion.'

'It must be hard for you. Can you tell me who you are?'

'A friend of your husband's.'

'Pleased to meet you.'

'Pà, there's something I need to confess to you.'

'Sorry, Maria, I don't have time to talk right now.'

'Pà, it's important.'

'Do you need something?'

'No, it's just that I got pregnant and I had an abortion.'

'There's no need for me to tell you what I think.'

'Please, tell me. There is a need.'

'You've known for years, Maria, what I think.'

'Tell me!'

'There's no need.'

'There is a need, Pà. Tell me!'

'It'll hurt you. Best not.'

Father, you're a stone.

Father, you're so naive to think that the wound is only fatal if the bullet is lodged in your flesh.

Father, you can pull it out with a pair of tweezers and take it to a lab and wait for the ballistics report, but there's still no answer because you don't have any weapons in your storeroom to compare it with.

Father, what should we do if there's an entry wound and an exit wound?

You tell me.

With plaster? With make-up? With a nail? Tell me, how do you stitch up a vacuum?

'Pà, say something.'

'Maria, what can I say? It doesn't surprise me. I think the plot, as in the best films, makes perfect sense.'

Pà, turn that damn screen off.

Is that enough? Really?

Really.

His mouth has vanished from his face.

'Rita, I need to tell you something.'

'You can say anything to Rita, Signora Maria. Rita is secret.'

'I got pregnant but I had an abortion.'

'Oh!'

'Tell me, what can I do now?'

'Sorry. There are some stains not even Rita can clean.'

'Ruth, I had an abortion.'

'How do you feel?'

'I don't know.'

'You'll know.'

'Gigi Fiore, when you were a kid, your sports bag was so embarrassing.'

'I know.'

'I had an abortion.'
'Well, I'm always really careful.'

'Nicola, there's something I need to confess.'

'Darling, do you fancy pizza tonight?'

'Yes, I do.'

'OK. So, Mary Mine, what's up?'

'I got pregnant but I had an abortion.'

His body starts to shrink, getting thinner and thinner.

His shoulders wither until they are a straight line.

His eyes turn into tiny dots.

His legs fold like a pleated fan.

All that's left of his laugh is the gap in the middle. Now it's a black hole.

Collapsing on himself with the elegance of a star that has provided heat and light until now and has run out of energy. Then he implodes and everything is dark.

This time the kitchen cupboard door does not make it. It falls off and can no longer be fixed.

Conclusions

If I go through with option 1, I'll lose custody of Antongiulio for sure. Nicola, who will have left me, will get full custody.

Luckily, with exemplary foresight, I'd have already mentally handed over the aforementioned imaginary dog to the American auntie.

Aside from this collateral damage, scenario 1 (I take the pills and tell everyone I've had an abortion) will be the last piece of the mosaic after twenty-five years' work, including all the confirmations and reassurances from all sides.

The pain will pass but coherence will win the day.

Coherence is without a doubt an admirable quality.

Nicola wouldn't resist this time, he would run out of question marks with all the reparations he would ask of me.

The prospect, at this point, compared to the Gigi Fiore debacle a year ago, is a wholesale massacre of the kitchen.

Evaluation

Though composed in the form of a dialogue, which was not expressly required by the title, the essay is well written and well argued.

Dramatic coherence has long been appreciated by the evaluating committee.

The student passes.

I archive the essay in my mind.

I'm cold.

I put the boots I'd taken off for no purpose back on.

My grandmother, my mother's mother, that is, has always told me that when your feet are cold, the rest of your body gets cold. Apart from when she got the words of a song mixed up, my maternal grandmother has never told me any lies. So it must be true.

Nonna, what would you do? And what about me?

There are still three pills, and they are still yellow.

This room is still horrible.

Maybe it's even smaller than before.

Not good.
I can't go on looking at my socks.
So I look at my boots.
Good.
I think some more.

Motherearth

In prayers, it's the father who's in heaven

Question 2
What happens if I don't take the pills?

Essay

I envisage a belly.

I envisage temporarily finding it hard to touch and/or see my feet.

I envisage carrying a separate life, like a real rucksack that you carry on your back, not one on wheels.

I envisage little kicks, which must be sweet.

I envisage Nicola lighting votive candles under the effigy of my body, bringing me succulent morsels and waiting for me to guzzle them under his gaze. Like a nurse on a psych ward with medication.

I envisage his mother, my mother, his sisters, my father.

All of them expecting.

And then she's born and then she's a girl.

And I call her Liberty, and I argue with everyone over the stupid name.

And luckily my grandmothers are dead so at least they aren't taking part in the discussion.

I envisage looking at her and finding her beautiful.

She's a baby penguin. Like me and Nicola. Stranded on ice, halfway between the kingdoms of sea and land, with an unrealistic ambition to fly.

If we have never learnt to use these vestigial, decorative wings, would we be able to teach her? Would we be able to show her how?

Or how to swim fast?

Could she learn on her own?

I envisage the shop, which I decide I'll keep in the end.

And Ruth, who doesn't answer my letter and never turns the key in the lock.

Our home, in the meantime, fills up with new, brightly coloured things.

Then, perhaps, our neighbours put their apartment on the market and we are able to buy it, so that we can expand our lives without moving an inch.

My mother weeps for joy. My father, too, maybe.

We may go back on trial, but he might drop the charges.

But the way he looks at me, my father, that is, he threatens to take everything away at my first mistake.

They're all waiting for it. My first mistake, that is. Proof.

I envisage yet another conventional approach to life.

A mere exposure to the facts that ends up with me forming second-hand opinions about things.

Having an abortion and telling Nicola I'd done it would

be the perfect way to leave him. But then I would never have met you, my daughter. How foolish to even think about it.

Now I'm holding you in my arms, Liberty, and you are the most alive thing I've ever touched.

I kiss you while you sleep.

It's so difficult to rock you with handcuffs on but I manage because you, my dear little girl, will never want for anything.

Because, for you, I accept the cage. Especially now that, thanks to you, I see it so well, so clearly it looks like a film.

Look, Liberty. Look at what life is.

The films, paintings, novels we love the most are the ones that remind us of real life.

And the days of our life we love the most are the ones that remind us of novels, paintings, films.

There's something the matter with us, Liberty, we look for the wrong things in the right places.

When you cry, I soothe you by walking.

And when I meet another woman in the corridor, I smile at her.

To tell her that she guessed right, that you and I are a team.

Certain that she will be cheering us on.

I'll stop your crying because your pain is my pain.

That's what love is.

I'll love you for ever, my little girl.

You'll have to forgive me, though, if you're so remarkable that in all this sea of love you manage to identify a droplet of hatred.

You're not mad. It's there.

And it's my fault and nobody else's if I let it out.

One drop is enough to sully everything, my beloved little girl, enough to change the name of the colour we're looking at.

My lovely little fruit, forgive me if I can't remember ever having loved anyone before you came along.

I should have done things in a different order, I know, rather than testing whether my iciness will melt on your delicate, white, unblemished skin.

Plants need the right amount of water: not too much, not too little.

Your father would want you to be an eagle, I see you as a dolphin.

But now I don't care, you decide. Just please don't be a penguin.

I love you and I'm sorry.

Your mother.

Conclusions

If I go through with option 2, I would certainly be given custody of Liberty.

She could plausibly be managed, especially since her future will be charged with potential, a supernova, not a black hole.

Option 2 (not taking the pills) would appear to conform to the parameters of good sense and the inexorable circle of life.

A dramatic turn of events is always appreciated, in films as much as in life.

Even more so when the turn leads events towards the much-hoped-for and clichéd happy ending.

The kitchen, and its units, would remain unscathed.

In fact, it would be bigger and better-used due to the multiplication of so-called mouths to feed.

Evaluation

Although this essay is composed mostly in an epistolary style, not explicitly required by the title, it is well-written and well-argued.

Heart-warming plot twist.

The commission has no choice but to confer top marks.

My feet are warm but it's still cold.

Isn't the hospital supposed to make us feel better?

Liberty, what would you do in my place? What should I do?

Mother-of-pearl

It's so hard to draw you freehand, Venus

Question 3

What happens if I don't take the pills and run away to the Caribbean?

Essay

Taking a plane when you're pregnant and flying to an exotic location would be great.

At airport security they let me skip the queue, smiling indulgently when they see my belly. The flight assistant leans over and asks if I want an upgrade to first class, I'll be more comfortable there.

They give me as much fresh orange juice as I want, in crystal champagne glasses, and a luxury pochette stuffed with miniature cosmetics.

I've chosen Santo Domingo as the birthplace of my son, Pedro.

We'll make it on our own, him and me. We'll swim in the ocean, speak two languages and never take the sun-drenched days for granted. We'll continue to be in awe of, and avoid being inured to, the absence of clouds.

As soon as I land, I'll look for a job that's right for me, a real job such as a schoolteacher or a journalist.

I'll love my baby without ever emotionally blackmailing him.

Pedro will never ask about his origins, who his grandparents or father are, or where he comes from, because he'll be really happy. And if you're really happy, there's no room for questions. We won't own a mobile phone.

Nicola will never come and look for me, and neither will my mother or anyone else.

My life, thanks to this new little life that needs looking after, will be reset to an eternal summer with no shady spots.

Conclusion

Never has any decision been wiser. Option 3 is shaping up to be a triumph of ease and independence.

Evaluation

The exam is declared invalid owing to imprecisions contained in the title that jeopardise the composition and lead to a further sequence of errors.

It is clear that the candidate cannot escape. Her passport has expired, her skin is too delicate to be constantly exposed to the sun, she has no qualifications that would allow her to gain employment of the nature she describes, there is no sign in her of a propensity for living in the tropics.

We apologise for any discomfort we have caused and invite her to write another essay on a topic of her choice.

The exam is annulled. Mark: unclassified.

The question is impossible to answer but we continue to hold the candidate in our esteem.

The walls have grown even closer.

They're even barer than before.

You need air to live.

This is certain, a statement that does not contain any errors.

My gaze falls on the pills.

The pills look like sweets.

The kind you chew on rather than swallow.

Malamadre

Es una herbácea perenne
Conocida también como lazo de amor

*F*_{*ree Title*}

What actually happens.

Essay

I've always wanted to be able to swim as fast as I think.

Summer definitely spoke as fast as she thought.

The speed of thought may not be as fast as the speed of light, but I find it amazing anyway.

This room is visibly shrinking, I swear.

You can't take a big decision in a small room.

There's not enough space to hold it.

I get off the bed.

I flatten the paper sheet I was sitting on with my hands, even though I know it will be thrown away.

It's a strange gesture I watch myself make. It's the sort of thing Nicola would have done. The man who takes the trouble to make his bed even in a hotel.

I open my bag.

In it, there's the list I wrote for Enrico. I take it out. I read the last line and I don't know what's hit me.

It must be the hormones, or because I'm hungry. That's what I think. Is this itch in a place that doesn't exist called hunger? I feel like scratching what is effectively an empty space, a hole, but my brain tells me not to go there. It tells me to bite.

Not the pills.

The pills aren't sweets.

You don't chew pills, you swallow them.

But it's not compulsory.

I can change my mind.

I do nothing but think.

My sister died because she was hungry. That's it!

Death, it seems, is something you swallow, something you take by mouth.

My sister died because she swallowed a piece of the building set, which led to destruction rather than construction. I hate it when words betray their meaning.

Swallowing these little yellow pills that look like sweets will take a future away.

They deny a hypothetical time period.

Death by swallowing.

Death stinks and flowers are needed.

This room is too small for all these thoughts. I can hear them bouncing off the walls and hitting me square in the face.

Like squash. Hit or duck. Otherwise it hurts.

I don't get why there are three little pills and not one big one.

Breakfast, lunch, dinner.

Why divvy the drug up?

Maybe so it can be swallowed more easily, to make the end a more comfortable experience.

I'm standing up.

The bed behind me and the door in front of me.

I'm rocking like a boat, shifting the weight of my body from foot to foot.

I read the last line of my note to Enrico: *Her birth chart. I have a friend who could do it for her and she might be able to help you in other ways.*

What if Ruth takes back what's hers?

I've been stealing lives all my life.

What if Ruth kept *Be Present!* and became the giraffe in the town zoo? That stupendous animal with a neck that is so absurd you wonder how it manages to resist the purely functional evolution of the species. Giraffes are so unbalanced, but so beautiful.

What would Ruth do in my place?

What would I do, if I were me?

I leave the list of gifts on the bed.

Another chip off the slab on my chest.

I leave it here in case Enrico needs an anchor to hold him down in order not to float away. I can't face him when he comes back. I can't let myself be looked at like that again, or be interrogated as if I were stupid.

I'll call him.

This room is really too small, too small for something so big.

I make for the handle and I'm scared the door won't open, that it's locked from the outside. Maybe, ultimately, that's what I'm hoping for.

Scratch that.

It opens.

I tread lightly on the shiny clean floor.

I'm scared I might dirty the tiles and make someone ill.

I head for the lift.

Lift going down.

It's so easy to find your way back the way you came, even when you don't know the route.

Maybe I can detect the smell of our previous passage, or maybe I trust the marble chips that I continue to scatter like fairy-tale breadcrumbs.

A doctor walks past with a stethoscope around his neck. He looks disgusted when he sees me.

I look down, my boots stepping, left, right, with my feet inside them.

It feels like everyone is staring. Like everyone knows.

I'm scared I'll meet the nurse from before. I'm scared I'll meet the woman with the little boy.

Let me out of here, please.

How long does the lift take to go down three floors?

Here's the Accident and Emergency door, opening automatically.

Which means it can sense my presence, which means I still exist.

I go out without looking back. You can learn a lot from Orpheus's mistakes.

Hunched over, I keep on walking fast until I get to the car park, where the bus dumped me earlier.

I look up. *Ciao*, sky.

My chest rises and falls fast.

Then it slowly calms down. Things are much better without walls.

It's still light because the days are beginning to get longer.

Ruth would be relieved.

I'm relieved, too.

There's the lightest of breezes, carrying with it the smell of the sea.

Mothertongue

Tempus fugit
tempest on its way

The hospital is right by the beach.

I switch onto autopilot, completely unaware of my feet as they continue marching of their own accord.

I once read that we're programmed to feel only one pain at a time.

So, if my feet were hurting in this moment, it would eliminate all the other pain that I feel spreading over my skin. But my feet resist, they're tough. Forget Achilles.

I'm there.

The sea is calm, like the one I dreamt about last night. Though, luckily, there are no falling rainbows in the vicinity.

There's not a soul in sight and it's clear why. We're always looking for the right things at the wrong time.

I walk to the shore and crouch down. I stick a finger into the water. It's freezing.

The sea and the sky are one and the same, no dividing line.

Light blue and pink pastels.

As if they can't decide, at sunset, whether life and the world are masculine or feminine.

At that moment, I remember that I need to find twenty-five pretty shells for poor Simonetta, who will be celebrating tomorrow the same anniversary I celebrated yesterday.

Equally tragic, given the husband she has ended up with.

I consider that the task doesn't make any sense, given that I have no intention of opening the shop tomorrow. Or the day after, or ever again.

But I start picking out the shells anyway, even though they serve no purpose.

I should do things that don't serve me more often. 'Serve' is a word that goes against the idea of liberty.

Sand in my boots.

Shells in my pocket.

Fossils.

Sediment.

Dolomites.

Layer after layer, the sea could turn into a mountain.

All you need is an earthquake or two and a long, long time to become something completely different, something new.

The point is that it's always to do with the recipe, not the ingredients.

The raw materials are the same, but you need to know how to mix them.

I'm an accumulation of flesh, bones, blood, nerves, muscles, organs.

I'm not a killer.

I never have been.

I'm not a killer.

I'm a little girl who was playing in her room.

I'm not a killer.

I'm a beach that, at a certain point, after years of pressing, compacting, silting, has turned into a mountain.

Taller even than a giraffe.

I want to go back to being the sea, I want to go back into the water, certain that it will recognise me.

I lick the finger I dipped in the water. Only a little, with the tip of my tongue, just to taste how salty it is, how undrinkable it is.

We're face to face, me and the sea.

I look at the water, scattering a chip of my precious block of marble for every blink of my eyelids. They are my ashes.

I'm crumbling, crumbling, and under the marble there's a compass, like Ruth's, that points north of where I want to go.

I'm not a killer.

I'm a woman who's dying of hunger.

I don't think I've had a teatime snack for more than twenty years.

Breakfast, lunch, dinner.

Then there are extras, which are like gifts, treats, harmless infringements of the rule.

I think tonight, before going to bed, I'll take my necklace off.

That way I can see what shape my neck is, if it looks longer.

I think tonight Nicola and I will eat a whole pizza each.

Maybe we can think about moving house.

Maybe to somewhere with a dishwasher.

Maybe there's another airport he could fly from.

Maybe London, or somewhere I don't know.

Maybe I could be an indie singer called Thin Air, or a publicist, or a poet specialising in compound words, or I could finish university.

Mix up all the ingredients again.

Or stay on this beach forever.

I imagine a table on this flat sea.

With a tablecloth on it, laden with all the food in the world.

I need to try them all again, one by one, because I really don't know which ones I like and which ones I don't.

Maybe ice cream is the most delicious thing in the universe and I've simply forgotten.

I imagine a rainbow, but this time it's not endangering humanity.

Nor is there treasure hidden under one of the two ends.

A normal, scientific rainbow made up of light, water and refraction.

I don't know what my favourite colour is. I think I need to look at them all again so that I can decide.

There are so many things I don't remember about myself.

I imagine digging and finding Nicola's heart, taking it to him as a gift.

Telling him that I lied, that I knew perfectly well where I'd buried it.

Giving everything back to everybody. Not holding onto anything that's not mine. However gradual and slow the movements of the universe, the evolution of the species, diseases, erosion and accumulation are, there's always a precise point when things cease to be what they are and become something else. There's always a passage that can be identified.

There's a precise point in the sea where, when you stretch your leg out, you can no longer touch the bottom.

It's completely dark.

Of course I had, I'd seen the sun set incredibly slowly, but darkness and light always come suddenly, like the train when it goes in and out of a tunnel.

I find my phone so that I can use it as a torch. There's another unintended use.

There are three missed calls from Enrico.

If he calls me in the next ten seconds, I'll answer. Otherwise, I'll call him back tomorrow.

… seven… eight… nine… nothing.

I sit on the beach. I'm really very tired.

I rummage in my bag until I find the pills.

I hold them in the palm of my hand.

There are still three of them. They are still yellow.

The sand is damp and I'm sure it'll stick to my trousers. The cheek!

My sister, unlike me, would have loved the feeling.

I send a text to my mother.

Mà, I need to confess something.

Double tick. In a second, as usual.

What is it, apricot?

I take my time tapping out all the letters. Autocorrect doesn't need to clear up any confusion created by my opposable thumbs.

I couldn't wait for Sunday. I opened the egg today.

There she is, faster than thought.

You did the right thing, sweetie. You must show me what was inside. Emoji with a kiss, emoji with a heart.

Nicola, Mà, Pà, Rita, Roberta, Lucia, Gigi Fiore, Ruth, World.

We have so many things to say to one another.

Would you like me to tell you that I'm pregnant and that we'll all be happy?

Would you like a + 1 in the population count? It would be a victory for you.

Would you like to clear your conscience with my daughter? With new hope? With a new life that fixes yours? You want reassurance.

Or would you prefer me to say that I had an abortion? Would you prefer a -1?

You would win either way, coming full circle and ridding yourselves of the pity you feel for me. Do you want to prove that you were right to stick a label on me all my life? You want to let yourselves off the hook in the trial and make me pay.

The truth is, there's another way.

The truth is that I'll never tell any of you what I'm about to do.

No. I'll never tell.

Get out of my head, all of you.

There's no room for you, or for any others.

Get out of my body, all of you.

There's me, the dark and the sea.

Big spaces, good for big decisions.

I close my eyes and listen.

There's only the sound of the sea.

I listen harder. I can't hear a thing.

I was looking for a heart. I can't hear a thing.

I'm not a killer.

I feel like laughing.

Maybe I should be crying.

I don't know how to.

Offspring

One day
light on our feet
you and I
will learn
the pas de deux

I clutch the pills in my right hand.

It's dark but I don't need eyes to see.

I swallow the pills.

It takes a while because I have to do it without water.
Seawater is no use.
The first. The second. The third.
I'm not a killer.
I don't want this baby.

THANK YOU

Tiziana Triana and Lavinia Azzone for their work, trust and harmony.

Aina Martí-Balcells for having magically brought these pages back to the country where they were born.

Clarissa Botsford for her profound insights.

Valentina Farinaccio for her phone call while I was in a waiting room, and for everything else.

Lori Albanese for all the splendour, advice and care.

Alessandro, who shouts from the rooftops of my imagination and makes me run fast.

Captain Gerardo De Maria for his advice on aeronautics.

Doctor Gaetano D'Ambrosio, my fantastic uncle, for his medical advice.

My friend Anna Povia, for her advice on psychomotricity and maternity.

My family.

The kitchen at Walters Close, London, where I wrote a big part of this story.

Dr Alice Dell'Erba for fresh light cuts.

Claudio Ongaro, my manager.

Those who listen to my music and the readers of *C'est la Mou*, with all my heart.

My father.

You, whoever you are, with this book in your hands.